## "Who are you, Maddie Williams?"

Jackson looked at his neighbor. It was not easy getting his youngest to eat vegetables.

Maddie muffled a laugh and shrugged as she dipped a tomato wedge into her pool of ranch.

His sister served up the salad for Dora along with ranch dressing, and sure enough, Dora dug right in. One veggie at a time.

His sister's comment about Maddie being good with the girls ran through his thoughts. Getting Dora to eat raw veggies was a huge win. It appeared that Maddie might be just what the girls needed.

He didn't want to think about his needs.

It was funny that the fascination with their neighbor had started out with a big gray parrot he'd been afraid to touch. Maddie was definitely different from the women he'd known, but similar in the one way that mattered most—she was way too attractive. Regardless of his sister's belief that she'd be good for him, Jackson knew that he could mess up this seemingly perfect situation if he didn't keep a cautious distance.

**Jenna Mindel** lives in Northwest Lower Michigan with her husband and their dogs, where she enjoys the Great Lakes, the outdoors and strong coffee. Her love of fairy tales as a kid paved the way for Jenna to eventually create her own happily-ever-after stories. Her passion grew into writing flawed characters who realize their need to trust God before they can trust each other. Contact Jenna through her website, www.jennamindel.com, or at PO Box 2075, Petoskey, MI 49770.

## Books by Jenna Mindel

### Love Inspired

### *Second Chance Blessings*

*A Secret Christmas Family*
*The Nanny Next Door*

### *Maple Springs*

*Falling for the Mom-to-Be*
*A Soldier's Valentine*
*A Temporary Courtship*
*An Unexpected Family*
*Holiday Baby*
*A Soldier's Prayer*

*Mending Fences*
*Season of Dreams*
*Courting Hope*
*Season of Redemption*
*The Deputy's New Family*

Visit the Author Profile page at LoveInspired.com.

# The Nanny Next Door

## Jenna Mindel

# LOVE INSPIRED

### INSPIRATIONAL ROMANCE

# LOVE INSPIRED®
## INSPIRATIONAL ROMANCE

Recycling programs for this product may not exist in your area.

ISBN-13: 978-1-335-58571-4

The Nanny Next Door

Copyright © 2023 by Jenna Mindel

For questions and comments about the quality of this book, please contact us at CustomerService@Harlequin.com.

Love Inspired
22 Adelaide St. West, 41st Floor
Toronto, Ontario M5H 4E3, Canada
www.LoveInspired.com

Printed in U.S.A.

There is no fear in love; but perfect love casteth out fear: because fear hath torment. He that feareth is not made perfect in love.

—*1 John* 4:18

I'd like to thank Karen Mazzoline and Heidi Mindel for their insight into teaching music, piano lessons and band. Also, a big *Thank You* to Lydia Westphal for sharing her wealth of knowledge in raising exotic birds.

Ladies, I appreciate your time and any errors made are my own.

# Chapter One

Maddie Williams stared out her kitchen window at the moving truck parked in the driveway of the house next to hers. Golden leaves fluttered in the October breeze as she waited for a glimpse of her new neighbors. She'd seen the Sold sign over a week ago. That house next door had been vacant ever since she'd moved back to her hometown of Pine in the Upper Peninsula of Michigan a few months ago. She'd toured the sprawling two-story, but it was too big for just her and Pearl. She'd bought the little bungalow next to it and had used most of her savings for the down payment.

"Got kisses?" Pearl, her thirty-year-old African gray parrot, perched on her shoulder.

Maddie obliged by planting a kiss on her light-colored beak. "Do you think our new neighbors will be nice?"

"Who's nice?"

Maddie chuckled when the bird whistled. "You are, Pearl. You're a nice bird. A pretty bird."

"Pretty bird."

Movement next door caught her attention once again. Two burly men exited the truck carrying a huge couch down the ramp. They reminded Maddie of her late husband, causing her to shiver. Stan had been nearly a foot taller than her five-foot-four frame. She really hoped those two men were movers and not her new neighbors. She'd had her fill of big, loud men, enough to last a lifetime.

She watched a few seconds more and then gave up. "Enough snooping. Let's get you some lunch."

"Peanuts?" Pearl cocked her head.

"Maybe one."

Her husband had hooked Pearl on dry roasted peanuts, which were not good for her. One or two on occasion wouldn't hurt, but he'd given her handfuls. It was a miracle the bird hadn't gotten sick or worse.

*So glad he's gone.*

Maddie closed her eyes as the guilt that always followed her relief surged. "Forgive me, Lord."

"Forgeeve," Pearl mimicked.

"I'm trying." Maddie peeked again at the house next door.

More items were moved in by the brawny men and then a third one exited the house. He appeared to be giving the others directions. Shorter and slighter in build than the other two, he had close-cut dark hair that was combed back off his face, making him handsome in a poetic-looking way. Like the perfect Romeo cast in a play, he was certainly sigh-worthy and a welcome sight. The two big guys were his movers.

Maddie thought Romeo a little formal for moving day, dressed in a blue button-down shirt, down vest and khakis. But then, he wasn't the one hauling in the heavy stuff. She kept watching him, until the man suddenly looked straight at her and waved.

Maddie ducked, sending Pearl flying with a squawk. "I'm an idiot."

"Idiot! Idiot!" Pearl continued to fly about the kitchen before landing on the back of a wooden high chair.

Maddie slapped her forehead. Ducking out of sight was something a twelve-year-old might do. She was twenty-five. "That'll make a nice first impression."

Pearl ignored her to preen.

Maddie made lunch of sprouts, raisins, and banana with some chopped almonds for the parrot, sprouts and Swiss cheese with almonds and mayo in a pita for her. Drawn to the activity next door, she took another peek out her kitchen window, but Romeo was gone.

*Oh well.*

She handed Pearl a dish of food on the high chair and the parrot immediately dug in, sending bits of sprouts tumbling to the floor. Maddie used a splat mat under the high chair for easy cleanup of whatever Pearl might drop. Her husband hadn't liked that, either. Feeding Pearl in the kitchen had been on his long list of no-nos. He'd often called Pearl a dirty bird, which was far from true. Maddie gave Pearl a soft mist shower and blow-dry every week.

Shaking off bad memories that still plagued her, Maddie lifted her sandwich in salute. "Bon appétit."

"Bone appy-teet," Pearl mimicked.

Maddie laughed and opened her laptop. She connected to the internet and checked her email, hoping for a job lead. She'd applied for a few work-from-home seamstress positions, but so far no takers.

She'd already exhausted the local sewing market. She'd cast her inquiries as far as the college town of Marquette, about half an hour northwest, but found nothing. No one needed a seamstress, and none of the higher-end boutiques were interested in her simple designs at this time.

A knock at the door was followed by her mother's voice. "Maddie, it's me."

"Hellloooo." Pearl flapped her wings.

"I'm in the kitchen."

Her mom went straight to Pearl. "Hello, pretty bird."

"Pretty bird. Pretty." The parrot tipped her head for a pet.

Maddie got up from the table. "Want some lunch? I just made a sandwich."

Her mother grimaced. "If I'd known you were eating grass clippings, I would have brought you a sub or something more substantial."

"Idiot!" Pearl squawked.

"Hey. That's not nice." After five years around Stan, Maddie was grateful that Pearl hadn't picked up more colorful insults.

"Who's nice?" The parrot whistled.

Her mother snitched a piece of pita and gave it to Pearl.

"You spoil her." Maddie gave her mom a hug. "What's up?"

Her mother shrugged. "Just checking in."

Maddie narrowed her eyes. Something *was* up. "You could have called for that."

"Let's sit down."

"Okay." This was serious. Maddie tried to dispel the sinking sensation in her stomach, but couldn't, especially when her mother reached for her hand.

"The Ladies Auxiliary is sponsoring the Veterans Day program at the high school this year. They'd like to give you a plaque in appreciation of Stan's service."

*Of course they would.*

Maddie's belly soured. Stan had been an excellent soldier, but a lousy husband. Posing as the grieving widow for a hometown paper photo opportunity made her queasy. What would they all think if they knew that Maddie had wished for her husband's death?

"Stan the Man." Pearl give a shrill screech and shook her feathers.

Her husband had gone by that nickname since they'd met in high school. Pearl had never trusted him, choosing to keep her distance. Too bad Maddie hadn't been so wise. She was young and fancied herself in love when she eloped right out of high school, right after Stan enlisted in the Marines. Both of them were only eighteen.

"I know this will be hard, but just think about it, okay?" Her mother patted her hand. "Stan grew up here too, and it would mean a lot to the community."

More guilt.

"I'll think about it."

"That's my girl." Her mom smiled. "Although, I need to know by the end of the week. Veterans Day is only a month away and we have programs to print."

Maddie nodded.

Since moving back to Pine, Maddie had noticed that Stan had become quite the hometown hero. His name had been etched onto the community monument in Veterans Park with the other fallen military personnel from the area. Not surprising, but it had still made Maddie do a double take when she saw it.

Stan had been her hero once, but over time, he wasn't. It wouldn't kill her to perpetrate the sham that had been her married life for a single event. She'd done it for so long, what was one more day? For the sake of her town, her mom and even Stan's parents, who'd no doubt come, she could do it again.

"I don't need to think about it, Mom. I'll do it." Once committed, Maddie wouldn't back out.

"Thank you." Her mom smiled. "Now, tell me, how are you?"

"Fine," Maddie fibbed. She hadn't found a job to fill

her time and thoughts, so she obsessed between guilt and anger.

Everyone in town thought she was fragile with grief and kept their distance. Even her mother tiptoed around her, but then, her mother was busy with her new husband of only eighteen months. It wasn't grief that plagued Maddie. She'd wanted her husband to die. And he did. So, what did that make her?

Jackson Taylor chuckled when his neighbor ducked out of sight. He didn't get a good look at her other than a mass of blond hair and glasses. Those big round frames could be seen a mile away, let alone the hundred feet that separated their homes. He'd meet her eventually, he supposed.

"Daddy, come look." His seven-year-old daughter, Zoe, grabbed his hand and led him into the house.

This was the first time his girls had seen the place, and so far, they loved it. He didn't really want a house this big or old, but the price was right, as was the turn-key condition. The two-story had recently been renovated in that modern farmhouse style that was popular on home shows. Jackson didn't mind the stark white or gray walls throughout; it matched his frame of mind pretty well. After closing on his home in Escanaba, he had some cash left over, which was a welcome surprise, so he couldn't complain.

"What is it?" he asked, but kept following.

"You'll see." Zoe pulled him along to the front entrance and stairway. She tapped on the wall at the base of the stairs and it opened, revealing a secret little room. A dark one.

Fear clutched his lungs, stealing air and thought for a second or two. He bent down to enter and shut the door, then pushed it back open easily enough. Still, he didn't like it. The image of one or both of his girls trapped inside that room chilled his bones. There wasn't a latch—a magnet, perhaps? He'd look into closing it off permanently.

He exited and knelt down so he could look his seven-year-old daughter in the eyes. "Don't ever hide in there. And never shut your sister in that little room."

Zoe took note of his serious tone and nodded.

"Thank you for showing me." He ruffled Zoe's hair.

His daughters had seen enough darkness in their short lives from the clinical depression their mother had battled and finally lost last year. He hoped moving forty miles north to Pine would give them all a fresh start. At the very least, it took them away from the whispers of his wife's suicide and the reproachful glances still cast his way.

He'd left the Escanaba high school to accept an open music teacher position at the Pine Middle School that included band instruction for the attached high school. He started Monday, only a few days away.

"I'm going to get us some lunch. Want me to take both girls with me?" Melanie, his sister, jingled her keys.

"I want to stay with you." Zoe tugged on the bottom of his vest.

Jackson smiled at his four-year-old, Dora, hanging close to his sister. She had her index and middle fingers in her mouth, something she'd picked back up after his wife's death.

"If you'd take Dora, that'd be great." He handed his sister a couple of twenties and then gently lifted his youngest daughter's chin, dislodging her fingers. "Be good for Aunt Mel."

Dora nodded.

"Thank you," Jackson said. "For everything."

His sister smiled. "This will work out, you'll see. Be back in a few."

As he watched them leave, he sure hoped so. Moving away from his family was a big step. Another was starting afternoon care for his youngest. He was on a waiting list at the daycare attached to Dora's preschool, but it might take a while to get her in.

Melanie had offered to watch her until then, but he didn't want to take advantage. Mel was willing to make the forty-five-minute drive one way from Escanaba, but that wouldn't work come winter.

He and the girls used to live only a block away from his sister and her husband. It had been relatively easy for Mel to take the girls after his wife's death until the school year was over and then again this fall. He already owed her a lot.

Jackson had spent the summer months alone with his daughters. They had spent nearly every day at the beach, but the memories of how much Delia had loved it there cut deep. And he'd spent many a night comforting his girls' cries for their mother. Jackson couldn't have made it through this past year without his sister's help.

His mom and dad had pitched in as well, but Jackson grew to loathe their God-has-a-plan comments. How could his wife's suicide be part of God's plan? Over and over, Jackson had questioned a God who could let his wife take her own life by overdosing on antidepressants. God never answered.

"I wanna see my room." Zoe raced for the stairs.

"Stay out of the movers' way," he called after her, but Zoe was already gone.

Jackson stared at the boxes scattered around the kitchen that were opened but still packed. Melanie had wanted to clean the cupboards before putting away dishes. He'd hired a cleaning crew before moving day, so he was pretty sure those cupboards were good to go, but he'd let his sister do her thing.

He stepped out the back door that led to an expansive backyard and made a mental note of the perfect place for a garden next year. The girls would like helping with that. Would they be healed up by then? Would he be used to raising his girls alone? Living alone, sleeping alone?

Jackson shook off the dreariness of his thoughts and focused instead on the beauty outside his door. The autumn color had already peaked in Pine, and the stiff breeze sent those red, yellow and orange leaves fluttering to the ground. Pine might be only forty miles north of Escanaba, but the elevation was higher and the winters saw more snow as well.

He'd miss living within walking distance of the beaches on Little Bay de Noc. His girls loved the Lake Michigan shoreline. His wife had too. Wrestling with the familiar stab of loss, Jackson went back inside to search for his daughter.

The movers had finished unloading the first-floor rooms; the second floor was next. He climbed the stairs and found Zoe in a large bedroom she'd share with her sister. She knelt by a window, looking out at the same view he'd been enjoying only moments ago.

"What's that?" Zoe pointed.

Jackson stepped closer. "What?"

"That white building."

There was a rectangle of a screened house with a slanted tin roof set up in his neighbor's yard. It looked rather narrow, and it also appeared to have small bare trees arranged inside.

"Huh. I don't know, Zoe. Maybe it's a cage of some sort." A big one.

"For a pet?"

Jackson shrugged. "Could be."

"Can we go see?"

He chuckled. "Not now. Come on. Aunt Mel is probably back with lunch."

"Then can we go?" Zoe slipped her hand in his.

"Maybe." They made their way downstairs.

He did want to meet his ducking neighbor and that'd be a good way to do it. Check out the mysterious screened structure in her backyard. He'd already met the elderly couple on the other side of him when he'd toured the house. They were nice folks.

Jackson liked knowing what kind of people surrounded his girls. He had checked every known register in Pine before looking at houses. Before he'd even accepted the music position. It turned out that Pine was a safe little community, nestled in the middle of nowhere.

"I saw your neighbor just now." Melanie pulled out wrapped sandwiches along with containers of soup and set them on the kitchen table. Then she handed out paper plates. "She's young and really pretty. She was walking this gray parrot into a large cage when I pulled in. It was pretty cool. I waved."

"Did she duck?" Jackson asked with a chuckle.

His sister gave him an odd look. "She waved back."

A normal response was always a plus.

"Can we go see?" Zoe jumped up and down.

"Maybe after lunch." Jackson gave each daughter half of a turkey sandwich, then looked at his sister. "That solves the mystery of the screened structure. Zoe could see it from her bedroom."

"Pretty bird," Dora mumbled through a mouthful of sandwich. His four-year-old's language had regressed a bit, along with some behaviors, such as sucking her fingers.

"Do you think we can pet it?" Zoe rocked in her seat while she chose a potato chip.

Jackson didn't like the idea of his girls touching a bird large enough for that screened cage. "Probably not. Birds aren't like puppies or kittens."

Melanie chuckled. "You won't know that until you go over there."

"Right." Sooner was probably better than later. If he had moved next to some kind of kook, he'd rather know that now. Or rather, after lunch.

Maddie heard a knock at her front door. Thinking it might be her mom returning because she'd forgotten something, Maddie didn't answer. Expecting to hear her mom's voice, she waited. Nothing came but a second knock.

"Coming." Maddie rushed to open the door and blinked.

Romeo from next door stood before her, and he was even more handsome up close. His eyes were bright blue and framed by dark lashes the color of his hair. He was taller than her but didn't tower, and she'd guess he was somewhere around thirty.

Looking down, she saw two little girls wearing matching pink jackets standing on either side of him. "Hello."

"Hi, I'm Jackson Taylor. We just moved in, or rather, we're still in the process. These are my girls, Zoe and Dora."

She spotted a wedding band on his finger and felt a momentary twinge of disappointment. She stepped back. "Would you like to come in?"

"My aunt Mel said you have a big gray bird," the taller girl piped up.

Was Aunt Mel the lady who had waved? Where was his wife? Maddie's curiosity only grew. She smiled to keep her mouth from blur ing out the questions running through her mind. "I do. Her name is Pearl. Would you like to meet her?"

The oldest, Zoe, she thought, had dark eyes that widened to the size of half-dollars. "Can I?"

Jackson coughed. "We don't mean to intrude. I just thought we'd introduce ourselves—"

"It's no trouble at all. Pearl is outside in her screen enclosure. We can walk around to the backyard if you'd rather." She waited for them to step back.

Only they didn't. In fact, Romeo looked wary, as if she'd hold them all hostage. The thought nearly made her laugh out loud.

"She's very gentle," Maddie added with a straight face.

"Please, Daddy?" Zoe begged. Her dark hair was long and straight. A beautiful kid.

"Please?" the younger girl, Dora, chimed in too. Her hair was lighter, with more waves than her sister's, and she had adorably chubby cheeks.

Their father looked torn and then finally gave in and stepped back. "Only for a moment. I really didn't mean to barge in."

"You're not barging—you're introducing. My name is Maddie, and you might as well meet Pearl. In case she ever gets loose, you'll know where she belongs."

Now he really looked alarmed. "Does she escape often?"

"Hardly ever." Maddie stepped outside and shivered. It might be mild for mid-October, but she tended to be cold, even in summer. She was glad for the thick sweater she wore. "Follow me."

Maddie led the way around the side of her house that

faced his. Only a narrow length of grass separated their paved driveways. Their garages were situated next to each other as well, a one-car stall for her while his held two. Their respective backyards were divided by a hedge of mature forsythia bushes that probably needed trimming since some branches had grown gangly. The hedge grew on Romeo's property, so that'd be up to him to manage. Not to mention that she had no idea how to trim one bush, let alone a whole line of them.

"Here she is." Maddie pointed toward the large screened avian enclosure complete with a slanted tin roof that could handle the snow load of the central Upper Peninsula.

"Hellloooo." Pearl flapped her wings.

"Wow," Zoe whispered.

Before opening the door, she turned. "It might be better if we enter one at a time."

"Can I go first?" Zoe asked.

Maddie tipped her head. "I think maybe your dad should go first, so he knows it's safe."

Jackson visibly paled. "Girls, we're going to watch from here."

"I grew up with Pearl. She's good with kids." Not as good with some men, but Maddie wasn't going to mention that. She believed that only Stan had ruffled her feathers.

"Thank you for the offer, but I'd rather we stay on this side of the screen."

"I'll go in and bring her closer for you to see." Maddie didn't want to push, especially since her neighbor appeared overly protective of his daughters.

"Did she belong to your parents, then? The bird," he asked.

"I inherited Pearl from my grandfather five years ago." Maddie went inside and closed the door just as Pearl came flying toward her. She held up her hand for the parrot to land.

She turned and saw both girls watching in awe. Jackson Taylor still held his daughters' hands and he kept them back from approaching too close to the screen.

"Pearl, meet our new neighbors," Maddie cooed.

"Who's nice?" Pearl bobbed her head and then lowered it.

"Wow." Zoe was entranced.

Her sister, Dora, smiled too.

Maddie was pleased that her parrot didn't seem intimidated or threatened by these new people, but then, she'd been socialized early and for most of her life.

"Hello there, Pearl." Jackson approached the screen slowly, keeping his voice soft.

"Hellloooo." Her parrot whistled and then tipped her head.

"What's that mean?" Jackson asked.

Maddie chuckled. "She's inviting you to pet her."

"Daddy, please?" Zoe squirmed away from her father's hold.

"No, honey." Then he asked. "Will she bite?"

"She doesn't normally, but like all animals, she can do things out of character if frightened." Maddie didn't confess that Pearl had bitten Stan several times.

Stan had deserved it and more. The last argument Maddie had with her husband, Pearl had dive-bombed him. She liked to think the parrot was trying to protect her. Every time her husband had reached for Pearl, the parrot retreated to the fan hanging from the cathedral ceiling of their town house.

Maddie had done her best to stand between them until finally her husband had stormed out of their military base home. He'd left for a training exercise the following morning and never came back.

More whistles and clicks and then another bowed head.

Maddie smiled. "She likes you."

"I'm honored." Jackson had a funny look on his face, as if he didn't quite believe a parrot was capable of preferences.

Zoe touched the fine wire screen, as if hoping to connect with Pearl.

"Do not touch." Jackson grasped her hand and backed them all away. "We'd better head home. We have a lot of unpacking to do yet. Thank you for showing us Pearl."

"Ah, yeah. Sure thing." She watched them walk away. The oldest girl looked ready to cry. Really, what was he so worried about?

"Kisses." Pearl tipped her head.

Maddie kissed her beak. "I wonder what's up with him."

Pearl whistled. "Idiot!"

"You might be right, Pearl." Maddie was sorry to admit that Romeo had lost a little of his shine.

The afternoon sun streamed in one area of the enclosure, and Pearl flew to perch in that sunny spot and preen. Maddie would leave her out for a while longer yet. There was no wind, and Pearl loved her outside time, even if it was a little chilly.

As she exited the aviary, Maddie wondered if she'd share a friendship with her new neighbors. Living so close, it would be nice, but then, she wouldn't hold her breath. Jackson seemed stuffy, but the girls were adorable.

She should reach out some other time and see what happened. Loneliness might be something she'd accepted in life, but she didn't like it. Especially now.

# Chapter Two

When Jackson made it back into the house, both girls were bawling. "Come on, you two. Stop with the crocodile tears."

Melanie stepped out of the pantry. "What happened?"

"D-Daddy wouldn't l-let us…pet Pearl," Zoe managed between hiccups and sobs.

His sister gave him a hard look.

"What?"

"It's just a bird, not some ferocious thing."

Jackson wasn't so sure about that. He didn't like the look of that big gray parrot with its eerie white eyes. Like something out of a Stephen King movie. "Have you seen its beak? The claws? We're not talking a little parakeet here." He raised his hand. "Nope, not touching it."

Zoe wailed and ran up the stairs.

"Movers done?" Jackson looked around. He'd noticed the truck had been gone when they returned.

Melanie sat down in a kitchen chair and lifted Dora onto her lap. "Yes. The invoice is on the table."

Jackson nodded as he reached for it.

"Aren't you going to comfort your daughter?"

"In a minute. She's angry more than anything." Jackson knew the routine. The drama. His oldest could play it to the hilt when she wanted to. "Huh, Dora. Sissy is mad."

Dora had stopped crying soon after Zoe left. She lifted her arms for him. "Uppy."

Jackson shook his head. He shouldn't reward her baby talk, but with that sweet face, he couldn't help it. Lifting his four-year-old from his sister's lap, he swung her around, delighted when she giggled.

"So, is your neighbor nice?" Melanie pulled coffee mugs from a box on the counter and put them in the cupboard.

He really appreciated her setting up his entire kitchen. "I suppose."

Jackson had definitely noticed how pretty Maddie was behind those big-framed glasses and baggy sweater. She was on the shorter side of average, blue-eyed with long blond hair and full bow-shaped lips—ah, yeah, way too attractive. It might be better if he stayed away from her. Her Stephen King parrot was a good reason to steer his girls away too.

"What's her name?" Melanie probed.

"Maddie. Didn't catch the last name."

"Married?"

Jackson looked up quick. "Why do you ask?"

His sister shrugged, looking too innocent to believe she didn't have an agenda. "Just curious."

"Well, I'm not. I don't know and I didn't ask."

"My, you're touchy." Melanie chuckled.

Jackson blew out a breath. He'd checked his pretty neighbor out thoroughly and felt guilty because of it. "I better look in on Zoe." He bounced Dora on his hip. "Let's go get Sissy."

"Yeah. Let's get Sissy," Dora chimed in her normal four-year-old voice.

He climbed the stairs, bouncing Dora the whole way, joining in with his daughter's laugh. In the hallway, he stopped when he overheard Zoe talking to her dolls. Their family counselor had said not to discourage it because Zoe may be more inclined to express her feelings to toys than to him. It wasn't something he liked hearing, but he'd abided by her advice.

That counselor was nearly an hour away now. At least they were down to bimonthly visits. They were doing well, all things considered, but would this move set them all back or move them forward? He wanted a normal life, and was a little added happiness too much to ask?

"I love my new room," Zoe explained to the stuffed mama elephant belonging to a family of dolls including a papa elephant and two little ones, just like their family used to be.

"It's big and has big windows. See?" Of all the dolls she had, Zoe talked most to the mama elephant. It broke his heart.

Jackson tapped on the opened door. "Are you still mad?"

Zoe looked at him, then turned away. "Yes."

He chuckled. Zoe wasn't stunted when it came to expressing herself or telling him a thing or two. He tossed Dora on one of the two bare twin beds.

Dora screeched with laughter. "Do it again."

He complied and was rewarded with more giggles. Even Zoe broke into a smile.

"Okay, enough of that." Jackson sat on the floor next to his oldest daughter. A box labeled *Stuffed Toys* had been opened. Other boxes lined the wall. He zeroed back in on Zoe. "I appreciate your curiosity when it comes to our neighbor and her parrot, but there is something to be said for being cautious."

His daughter tipped her head but wouldn't look at him. "Do you know what I mean by *cautious*?"

She shook her head.

He crossed his legs and considered how to best explain his reservations toward the woman next door and her horror-movie bird. "Sometimes, it's better to wait and make sure the person and her pet are safe before rushing in."

He had Zoe's attention. Dora's too. She had climbed off the bed and had come to sit in his lap. "There's a saying that *only fools rush in*. We do not want to be foolish, when we can be cautious."

"Why?" Zoe asked.

"What if I let you inside that big bird cage and the parrot hurt you? What would Maddie do? Would she have to give it away because it injured a little girl? You don't want something like that to happen, do you?"

"No." His daughter looked thoughtful. She was piecing it together.

"So, let's get to know what kind of person our neighbor Maddie is, before trusting her and her pet parrot. Can we do that?"

Zoe looked skeptical, but understood what he was saying. For seven, she was pretty sharp. With a thoughtful expression, she finally asked, "How are we supposed to get to know Maddie?"

*Sharp* didn't begin to cover it. Jackson had been effectively called out by his seven-year-old. "Well, I'm not sure, but maybe after we're settled in, like once we get your room arranged, I'll know how."

"That'll be forever."

"Not that long, I promise." Jackson tucked Zoe's thick straight hair behind her ear.

He had just promised they'd get to know their attractive young neighbor eventually. The one he'd wanted to stay away from because she was too pretty for his own good. The key word was *eventually*, and they had time on their side.

*Only fools rush in.*

Jackson had learned that lesson the hard way with his wife. He'd fallen for Delia so fast that he'd missed the signs of her issues. He'd simply thought her overly emotional. They'd sought help together once Zoe was born and things were good, but after Dora—something inside Delia had snapped. In spite of changing meds, her moods could plummet so quickly. Some days, Jackson couldn't break through to her, and then some days, she was fine. He'd never thought she was capable of—

Jackson should have known. He should have been more prepared, but she'd seemed so much better toward the end. Who knew what really went on inside someone's head? Inside their heart and soul.

He knew exactly what went on inside of him. He was mad at God. Despite his anger, Jackson missed the comfort brought by having faith in something greater than himself. And he missed having a wife—

*Nope.*

He couldn't go there, not for a very long time. Women should be off-limits in his life. He had two girls to raise and the stakes were just too high. The consequences were too hurtful when something went wrong.

The next day proved to be mild and sunny, so Maddie took Pearl outside to her enclosure once again. "Have fun."

The parrot flew to her favorite perch in a sunny spot and preened.

"I'll be back. 'Bye." Maddie exited the aviary.

"'Bye, 'bye," Pearl responded and then whistled.

Maddie entered her garage and fetched a rake. Donning work gloves, she walked to the far side of her front yard and began raking leaves. It wasn't long after she had a nice pile that she heard a young voice call out.

"Hi, Maddie." Zoe Taylor waved, her sister beside her.

Maddie waved back. "Hello, Zoe and Dora."

The younger girl ran across their parallel driveways to stop in front of her. Dora looked up with an impish smile that stole her heart. "Maddie, come play."

Maddie spotted Jackson Taylor bearing down on them before she could answer.

"Dora, you can't run off like that." Jackson looked frazzled as he trotted up to her as well.

Zoe followed. "Is Pearl outside?"

"She is." Maddie smiled, but knew better than to invite her to have a look.

"Can you play wif us?" Dora asked again.

Jackson scooped up his younger daughter. "Sorry. I'm trying to organize my garage."

"No worries." Maddie couldn't care less about her leaves. "What are you playing?"

"Hopscotch. Daddy drew it for us," Zoe answered.

"Well, that sounds like fun." It really did. She glanced at Jackson. "I could keep your girls occupied for a bit while you work in your garage. I'm pretty good at hopscotch."

He looked hesitant. Either he was nervous, cautious or the stuffiness had returned tenfold. Maybe he thought it silly for a grown woman to want to play with little girls. But finally, he smiled. "Actually, that'd be great, if you don't mind."

He had a really nice smile. Maddie hoped Jackson's hesitation was a simple case of not wanting to overstep instead of thinking she was weird. "I don't mind at all."

Dora squirmed out of Jackson's hold and promptly grabbed Maddie's hand. Zoe latched on to her other hand.

"We have lots of chalk," the older girl explained.

"Maybe we can draw afterward." Maddie was in no hurry to get back to her leaves. On such a warm autumn morning, indulging in some driveway chalk art sounded lovely.

"Yeah, draw." Dora stuck her two fingers in her mouth.

Maddie glanced at Jackson, but he stared straight ahead. His back was ramrod straight as well. Dressed in jeans today, Romeo might look more casual, but his manners were still pretty formal. Stuffy.

Once on her neighbor's driveway with better pavement than her own, Maddie spotted the drawn squares for hopscotch and the metal washer the girls were using as their marker.

"You can go first." Zoe handed her the washer.

Maddie tossed it into the first box, then leaped to the second box and onward. Turning at the end, she hopped back and picked up the washer. She tossed it into the second box and repeated her moves all without touching a line.

At this rate, the girls would never get a turn, so on her third round, she made sure that she landed on a line.

"Your turn." She handed Zoe the washer.

"You're pretty good." Zoe tossed the washer into the first box.

"I played a lot." Maddie missed those honest days when she was a kid.

She didn't have to hide who she was back then. Everyone in Pine knew her dad had left her and her mom. She'd grown up hearing that she and her mom were better off without him, but Maddie had often wondered if that were true. She'd had the stable influence of her grandfather, but that hadn't prevented her from running away to marry Stan.

Dora gave up before taking a turn at hopscotch. She lay on the driveway, coloring a flower with yellow chalk. It was a messy-looking thing with chalk scribbled outside the lines.

Zoe made four passes up and back before landing on a line, losing her turn.

"Dora, do you want to try?"

"Nope." The little girl kept coloring.

"Okay, I'll color too." Zoe grabbed a piece of blue chalk.

Maddie chuckled as it looked like their game was over. She peeked into the garage to see how Romeo had fared with organizing the space.

A large blue Subaru was parked in one bay, all neat and tidy. In the other bay, boxes were opened and scattered as if a second car didn't exist. There didn't seem to be a Mrs. Taylor in spite of the ring on her neighbor's left hand. Did he have full custody of his kids? But if divorced, why would he still wear a ring? There had to be a sadder reason Jackson parented alone. Just the thought pinched her heart.

He arranged a bunch of beach gear into a tall locker that looked far too narrow to hold everything. Fold-up beach chairs, umbrellas and sand toys. He was settling what looked like a picnic basket on the top shelf when a bunch of foam noodles cut loose and toppled out of the locker, bringing the umbrella out to crash onto the floor.

Maddie stepped closer. "Do you want some help?"

Jackson whipped around, then shrugged. "This might not be the best place for this stuff."

Maddie entered the garage. "Not many beaches around here. A couple of swimming holes and a small lake, but if you want a really good beach, you'll have to drive north to Marquette or Au Train."

"Or south to Escanaba, where the Bay is warmer." He didn't look at her, but kept trying to shove everything in that locker.

"There too." She'd picked up the foam noodles and handed them over. "Is that where you're from?"

"Yes."

Curious, Maddie asked the obvious question. "What brought you to Pine?"

Jackson's expression closed even more. "I took the open music position at the middle school."

"Oh, nice. Do you play any instruments?" Maddie wondered why he'd move to a much smaller town to teach in a smaller school. It couldn't be about money.

"A few woodwind instruments and the piano." His gaze finally met hers.

"That's impressive." Maddie couldn't play anything musical or read music, but she did love to sing. She'd been known to belt out a song in the shower and she sang along to the tunes she played in the car.

The umbrella chose that moment to fall out of the locker once again. She and Jackson went to catch it at the same time and bumped shoulders.

"Oops, sorry." Maddie took a step back and slipped on one of the foam noodles that had also fallen. She flailed but was caught and steadied by a pair of surprisingly strong hands at her waist.

"You okay?"

Once righted, Jackson let her go as if she were a hot coal. And she might as well be a burning ember, because her middle felt on fire, even through her thick sweater. Her face too. "Ummm, yeah."

"Maddie, do you want to color?" Zoe called from the driveway.

She glanced at Jackson to see if he reeled from their brief contact too, but he had stooped down to collect the foam noodle. Now she really felt like a dork.

"Coming." Maddie made her escape to the driveway.

She sat down on pavement warmed by the sun, grabbed a piece of pink chalk and started drawing. What on earth had just happened? One more peek into the garage showed Jackson rearranging that locker. He didn't seem the least bit affected by their awkward exchange, as if nothing had happened.

*Nothing did happen.* Maddie nearly laughed at her overreaction to Romeo's touch.

He'd given up on using the tall locker, opting for the hanging rafters overhead. Jackson slipped those pesky foam noodles and beach umbrella up and out of the way with the help of a stepladder. He caught her gaze and held it for a split second before looking away.

Pulse racing, Maddie let out the breath she'd been holding. No way should she entertain an attraction for her handsome neighbor. Obviously, he had an intriguing story, and raising two girls on his own dug into her soft spot pretty deep.

Maddie had blown it when it came to love and marriage, and she didn't deserve a second chance. Looking down, she noticed what she'd drawn. Feeling her face flush once again, she couldn't believe she'd made a big fat heart.

After half an hour or so, Jackson scanned the driveway. The three of them colored in vines and flowers and hearts that he suspected Maddie had drawn. Both daughters were captivated with their pretty neighbor and he couldn't blame them. There was something magnetic about her. No matter how hard he'd tried not to notice her, awareness of her every move mocked his effort. It didn't help that he'd found a very trim waist under the billowy sweater she wore.

Jackson stepped out of the garage and his stomach growled. "I'm going inside to make lunch."

No response.

He walked over to stand in front of his little artists and the woman who inspired them to concentrate so closely on coloring. Thinking on what he'd promised Zoe only yesterday about getting to know their neighbor, Jackson went out on a limb. "Maddie, would you like to stay for lunch?"

It was the least he could do for her time.

She looked up and her big round glasses had slipped down her nose. Her blue eyes were winged with dark liner, giving her an appealing cat-eye look.

He let his gaze linger.

She quickly pushed the glasses back in place. "Ummm, sure. Can I help?"

"I got it. Just sandwiches and chips, nothing fancy. Is there anything you're allergic to or don't like?"

"No. I pretty much like everything."

"Great." Jackson turned to go, hesitated and turned back around. "Thank you for doing this."

She smiled. "My pleasure."

For a second, he couldn't breathe. With sunlight shimmering in her hair and a wistful expression on her pretty face, Maddie reminded him of a princess in one of Zoe's storybooks. The one locked in a tower, waiting for true love to set her free. He shook off that crazy comparison and hurried inside before he got any ideas about becoming her prince.

Once in the kitchen, he went about gathering the ingredients to make four sandwiches. Peanut butter and marshmallow fluff for his girls, and the last of the turkey and Swiss cheese for himself and Maddie.

He peeked out the opened kitchen window at his girls and their neighbor. The three of them chatted happily about which colors to use. Maddie even instructed Zoe on shading techniques with chalk. He had to admit the drawings were well-done.

What did Maddie do for a living? An artist, maybe? He hadn't noticed her leaving her house at any particular time, and even if today was her day off, yesterday was a Thursday and her car had been parked in the same spot all day. He'd noticed because she drove a Subaru like him. Although, her car was a smaller model than his.

Maybe his neighbor worked from home. A lot of people did these days, including his sister. The idea of Maddie watching Zoe and Dora crossed his mind. The girls liked her. Should he consider it? Not until he knew her better.

And there was still that bird.

His words about fools rushing in came back to bite him. He might not have the time to wait. Dora needed care after preschool. Central UP winters often came early, and he didn't want his sister traveling in bad weather, especially after dark. Maybe he'd talk with Mel and get her thoughts on Maddie.

Stepping out onto the side porch, Jackson cleared his throat. "Lunch is ready."

"Can we eat out here?" Zoe asked.

"Oh, but we'll want to wash our hands," Maddie pointed out as she stood. Her fingers were covered in chalk dust. "Let's go inside."

Relief swept through him. He didn't want to drag

everything outside only to drag it all back inside. Plus picnics seemed too intimate.

Zoe shrugged and popped up. "Okay."

Dora slipped her chalky hand into Maddie's as they walked toward him.

Jackson got the distinct feeling that what he saw was right. That this woman next door was right for his girls. He shook off the sensation, downplaying it merely as wishful thinking. It wasn't as if God had whispered through his heart. He and the Lord were no longer on speaking terms.

Jackson hadn't really prayed since finding his wife dead. Oh, he'd yelled his fair share at God for not listening to his constant pleas. If He had, then maybe his wife might still be alive and she'd be whole.

"Which way to wash our hands?" Maddie asked.

Jackson stepped back inside. "There's a powder room just before the stairs."

"Great, thanks."

"I'll show her." Zoe skipped ahead of them.

Jackson noticed that Maddie left the door open while the three of them washed their hands in the half bathroom. He could hear the giggles of his girls and it ripped his heart open. They deserved better than losing their mom. Despite Delia's challenges, she had loved their girls.

Hearing the water shut off, Jackson got busy setting paper plates on the table, along with a big bag of potato chips. Next, he set two glasses of milk down for the girls, then turned to fetch a couple of cans of pop. He spotted Maddie standing in the middle of the kitchen looking lost.

"Have a seat. What would you like to drink?" He reached back in the fridge and pulled out root beer and cola.

"Water is fine." Maddie sat down.

Dora inched her chair closer to Maddie and then climbed into her booster seat.

Zoe sat down and reached for her sandwich.

Jackson handed Maddie a cold bottle of water, chose root beer for himself and then sat down as well. "So, what do you do for work?"

Maddie pushed her glasses up the bridge of her nose. "I'm currently looking. I like to sew, but no one needs a seamstress locally."

"Huh." He'd never heard of anyone sewing for a living, unless they worked in a factory. Still, she needed a job. Should he ask? She'd have to agree to a background check before he'd let her watch his girls. He should get his sister's input too. Melanie was a good judge of character, and she'd be back next week.

"Have you lived here long?" he asked.

Both his girls munched on chips, listening.

Maddie hadn't touched her food yet. "I grew up here, but moved back in June."

"From where?" Maybe, if he'd stop peppering her with questions, she'd eat. He took a bite of his sandwich.

"Camp Lejeune, North Carolina." Maddie folded her hands and bowed her head before she took a small bite of her sandwich.

Jackson stopped midchew. It was only a couple of seconds, but she'd just prayed over her food. Was she a believer, then? Another good sign. Even if he'd lost his faith, he appreciated that quality in others.

He used to say grace with his daughters at dinner. Nighttime prayers too. Shame kicked him hard. It wasn't fair to cut his girls off from such rituals because he was mad at God.

Maddie looked up, her face devoid of emotion. "My

husband was a Marine. He got killed while on a training exercise in February of this year."

Jackson's jaw dropped. "I'm so sorry."

"Our mommy died from taking too much medicine," Zoe added.

Maddie's gaze sought his.

"Around this time a year ago." Zoe might have spilled the beans, but Jackson didn't want to hide that his wife had taken her own life. It wasn't something he'd advertise either, but still…

He watched Maddie's eyes fill with tears, fascinated by the way she seemed to offer comfort by staring. If she started crying, the girls might join her and then he'd be in a real mess, but he couldn't think of a single thing to turn the subject around.

"Do you want some potato chips?" Zoe held out the bag.

He could have hugged his daughter.

"Ummm, sure." Maddie finally looked away. She reached in the bag and pulled out a couple of chips. "I'm very sorry."

"Yeah, me too." Jackson took another bite of his sandwich.

An awkward silence settled over them. All Jackson could hear was the crunching of potato chips. Until Maddie stood, her wooden chair scraping against the vinyl plank flooring.

"Mind if I take this with me? I have an appointment I nearly forgot and I need to put Pearl back inside."

"Sure, go ahead."

Maddie wrapped her half of a sandwich in her napkin. "Thanks for lunch. 'Bye, Zoe. 'Bye, Dora."

His girls waved, still munching.

"Can you come back tomorrow?" Zoe asked.

Maddie cast him an uncomfortable glance.

He found himself hoping so too. "We'll see, Zoe. Thanks, Maddie."

"Jackson." Maddie nodded and left.

He couldn't get the rich tone of her voice saying his name out of his head. Did she sing as well as draw? If so, he'd love to hear her while he played piano. Not a good idea. His next-door neighbor just got a whole lot more attractive and that was dangerous.

# Chapter Three

Maddie checked her watch. She might make it. She rushed to put Pearl back inside and the parrot squawked at her. "Sorry, but I have to run."

She placed Pearl in her cage complete with toys, perches and bells, and gave her a chunk of her sandwich before putting it in the fridge. "'Bye, Pearl."

"'Bye, 'bye."

Maddie rushed to her car. How could she have forgotten lunch with Erica and Ruth? Ruth Miller and Erica Laine were the only real friends she had in Pine, and she'd nearly blown them off. She looked forward to their lunch dates all week. But that was before an incredibly handsome man with two adorable girls moved in next door. This was all Romeo's fault. He'd really knocked her off-kilter.

She started the engine and backed out of her driveway but had to wait for a car to pass. Maddie peeked next door. Sure enough, Jackson was in the kitchen window. He didn't look up, giving Maddie the chance to appreciate the straight line of his nose to the narrowing of his chin. His wife had died only last year.

Maddie's heart pinched. She'd never forget the matter-of-fact way Zoe had explained how her mother had passed. Was it an accidental overdose or suicide? Either was awful. Both were heartbreaking.

She backed out and took off, driving a short distance to the Pine Inn Café. Once parked, she dashed inside. She'd had friends from high school who were still in Pine, but they had kids and families, and Maddie hadn't clicked with anyone she reconnected with.

Erica and Ruth were also recently widowed, and Maddie had met both in a grief support meeting at church. The group was small and awkward, so they decided to get together on their own. Both Ruth and Erica were older and wiser than her. Where the support group didn't quite meet Maddie's needs, these lunch dates filled the gap with honest conversation.

At least, Erica and Ruth were open, while Maddie still held back. Not sharing her true feelings was a habit she'd learned while married. She'd never wanted to upset the apple cart of Stan's mercurial moods. He could be downright nasty when he wanted to be.

Her relationships in Pine were few and surface level, much like those on the military base where she and Stan had lived. Back then, she'd worried whatever she said would make its way back to Stan. So, she'd kept a safe distance with people. It was a tough habit to quit.

Spotting Erica and Ruth seated at their usual table by the back window, Maddie waved.

They both waved back.

"Hi," she said as she sat down. "Sorry I'm late. How are you both?"

"Good," Ruth said with a smile. "We haven't ordered yet."

Maddie was happy to see Ruth smile. She'd secretly married her late husband's rich cousin in order to save her business and home from foreclosure. Disaster had been averted and Ruth seemed to get along well with the guy.

"How are you?"

Maddie squirmed under Erica's direct gaze. The woman was twenty-three years her senior and could see way too much in Maddie. More than Maddie's own mom. Once again, she deflected. "My new neighbors moved in."

"Have you met them?" Ruth asked.

"I have. A widower with two adorable young daughters." Maddie looked down at the menu, fearing what her eyes might reveal. Feeling her cheeks heat, she was sunk.

"He's young, then," Erica stated. "Interesting."

Maddie nodded and reached for her glass of water. "He's a little protective. He wouldn't go near or let his girls close to Pearl."

Ruth shrugged. "Maybe he's not good with pets."

"Maybe so." Maddie stared at the menu. She never knew what she wanted, and it didn't help that she'd already eaten half of a sandwich.

Erica usually went with the special of the day and Ruth ordered the same salad plate. In the six weeks they'd been meeting for lunch, Maddie had a hard time choosing almost every time. She really needed to be more decisive. She needed to be more of a lot of things.

"Any news on your job search?" Ruth asked.

Maddie shook her head, finally shaking off the effects of her secret Romeo next door. "Nothing. It's so disheartening. I'm doing okay with my widow benefits, but I'd rather stay busy, you know?"

"You could take college courses," Erica offered. "There's a shortage of nurses."

"No way. I'm terrible in emergencies and can't handle blood." Maddie admired Erica for her long career as an

RN. One she'd left to care for her ailing husband until he passed, soon after Stan. "Something will turn up."

"It will." Erica smiled.

Once their order was placed and then arrived, they bowed their heads and prayed over their food and then for the right job for Maddie. She didn't think God would grant such a request. How could He? Maddie had grown to hate her husband, and good Christians didn't hate their spouses. Scripture directed them to love one's enemies and pray for those who persecuted them. Maddie had failed on all fronts.

*Forgive me, Father.*

She had asked so many times, but she didn't feel forgiven. She didn't feel heard. She didn't feel much anymore—nope, not true. She'd felt Jackson Taylor's touch in the garage. The warmth of his hands on her waist stayed with her still. So did the sadness in his eyes when Zoe voiced how her mommy had died.

"Maddie, you okay?" Erica squeezed her hand.

"Yes. Why?"

"You were shaking."

Maddie withdrew her hand and proceeded to rub her sweater-covered arms. "Just cold."

Erica and Ruth exchanged a look.

"What? I'm always cold." Which was true.

Erica touched her shoulder. "We're both concerned about you. It's like you're holding everything inside, and that's not healthy."

"I'm just…" Maddie experienced the familiar twinge of guilt and said no more.

Ruth and Erica didn't know that she had wanted Stan to die. No one knew. She wished she could unload that secret and be done with it, but feared their reactions. They'd both loved their husbands. It was awful, shameful even. Still, she should give them something. "I don't know how to explain it other than to say my marriage wasn't an easy one."

"Marriage never is." Erica shook out her napkin. "I never bargained on being my husband's caregiver the last three years of his life."

Maddie nodded. "I'm so sorry."

"Yeah, me too," Ruth added.

Erica touched her hand. "I sometimes struggle with the relief I feel, but it's natural. Maddie, it is okay if you're relieved to be out of an uneasy marriage."

Maddie nodded. *Relief* didn't begin to cover it.

Her thoughts went back to her neighbor and the haunted sorrow she'd seen. There were so many hurting souls. Why should God forgive her, when there were others who deserved His grace and comfort so much more?

Late Monday afternoon, Jackson came home from a long first day. Between his classes, lessons, band practice and settling into his music room, he'd had a full day. But it was a good one.

"Hey, Jackson, we're in here." His sister folded clothes on the kitchen table with the help of Zoe and Dora.

"Daddy!" Both girls ran at him for hugs.

"You don't have to do our laundry." He scooped up Dora and noticed blue-and-white-checked curtains hanging from the windows. He touched the set over the big farmhouse-style sink. "Where'd you get these? They look nice."

His sister shrugged. "I had them. I thought they'd go well in here and give a shot of color. And it's no problem to do laundry. How was your first day?"

"It was good, actually." He spun Dora around until she squealed. "I need to update lesson plans, but I'll get there. The band is a little behind. They are playing for an upcoming Veterans Day Program held in the auditorium. The patriotic songs were chosen in advance by the guy whose job I filled, so it's a matter of getting the scores right."

"Will you get it done in time?"

"I think so." He knew how to press kids to improve. Get their buy-in on why it was important, and more times than not, they'd do the work.

Jackson put his daughter down and headed for the fridge. Opening the door, he scanned the contents. Plastic containers that were not there this morning sat stacked neatly on the middle shelf. Pulling one out, he opened the lid to reveal oatmeal cookies.

He glanced at his sister, before taking a few. "Thanks for these."

"Mom made them. There's chocolate chip too."

He let the homemade cookie melt in his mouth before shoving in another. "These are so good."

His sister laughed. "You really shouldn't talk with your mouth full."

He shrugged and then turned to Zoe and Dora. "Girls, could you go in the living room? I need to talk to your aunt Mel."

Zoe stared at him for a second or two, then pulled her little sister along. "Come on, Dora. Let's watch TV."

"What's up?" Mel asked.

"I need a favor." Jackson waited until he heard the TV. Zoe knew which cartoons were off-limits and switched the channel.

"Sure."

"I'm thinking about asking Maddie next door to watch Dora after preschool and Zoe when I have to stay after school, but I need your opinion." Jackson poured himself a tall glass of milk.

"That's a great idea. She's so close and—" his sister grinned "—Zoe told me all about her coming over to play and have lunch. Nice move."

Jackson reached for a towel to fold. "It wasn't a move. Dora ran over to her. Look, she's good with the girls and she prays over her food."

Mel arched her eyebrows and took the towel from him. "Not with cookie-crumb fingers. Eat. You can fold later."

Jackson slumped into a chair. "While you're here, would you check her out and let me know what you think?"

His sister cocked her head. "That's going to cost you."

He chuckled. "How much?"

"I will reach out to your neighbor on one condition."

Jackson wasn't sure he liked the sound of that. "And that one condition?"

"I take the girls over there to meet the parrot."

Jackson considered her terms. He wouldn't be surprised if Zoe had been after Melanie to do that very thing. He trusted his sister, and since that white-eyed bird gave him the creeps, it might be best if he wasn't there.

"Okay, it's a deal. The sooner the better." Jackson felt like he was getting the bargain end of the compromise.

Mel nodded. "We'll go tomorrow."

Jackson bit into another cookie. If Maddie didn't pan out, he didn't have a plan B other than the daycare waiting list. When he put Dora's name in, he'd been told it could take some time for an opening. They had strict student-to-worker ratios to maintain.

At least Zoe could go with him to the band room on the days he had rehearsal after school. She was good at entertaining herself. When his wife had been down, Zoe had learned to steer clear. She'd even looked after Dora, but he couldn't have his seven-year-old watch her baby sister in the band room. It wouldn't be fair to Zoe, and it would be distracting for him. But it was a last resort.

Normally he'd pray over something like this. Part of him still wanted to—the part that wanted to believe there was a God worth trusting—but then his anger reignited. God had let him down. God had let his girls down, and for that, Jackson wasn't sure he could forgive.

A knock on her door late in the afternoon surprised Maddie. Rain had kept her from raking leaves Monday and today. Peeking out the window, she spotted three figures standing in the drizzle. Two little and one big. Her heart pumped a little faster. Her neighbors!

Maddie smiled as she opened the door, but it wasn't Jackson standing with his girls. It was the woman who'd waved the other day. "Hi."

"I'm Melanie, Jackson's sister. I hope you don't mind us dropping in like this."

"Not at all. I'm glad to meet you. Come in." Maddie wasn't used to getting company other than her mother. "I needed a break from searching for jobs online. Here, let me take your coats."

"We want to meet Pearl." Zoe's brown eyes were big and hopeful as she slipped out of her school-bus-yellow rain slicker.

"You do?" Maddie hung the slicker on one of the hooks in her entrance and glanced at Melanie. "Is that okay? I mean, your brother didn't want them close to Pearl."

"I've got his permission." Melanie grinned as she hung her raincoat on a free hook, then helped Dora out of her slicker. "Off with your boots too, girls."

"Well then, come meet Pearl." Maddie wondered what

had changed his mind. Turning to Melanie, she asked, "Can I offer you something to drink or eat?"

"We had a snack when we got home from school, huh, girls?" Melanie kicked off her shoes too.

"We had cookies." Dora grinned. Some of the crumbs dusted the corners of her mouth.

Maddie chuckled. "Yum. I love cookies."

"If Pearl is supposed to be in her cage, the door's open." Melanie pointed into the living room.

"She's in the kitchen. She's out, so I'll head in there first. Just don't make any wild movements with your arms, okay?"

"Sure thing." Melanie grabbed the girls' hands and they followed Maddie slowly and carefully into the kitchen.

"Pearl, you have visitors." Maddie held up her hand. "Come, Pearl."

"Helllloooo." Pearl flew toward her and landed on her hand.

"Wow. She's beautiful," Melanie said.

Maddie brought Pearl close in front of her and smoothed her head. "She really is. If you'd like to pet Pearl, come up one at a time and be super gentle."

"Can I go first?" Zoe stepped forward.

"Yup. Don't be afraid. Touch her like this." Maddie showed her how to use the back of her finger to pet the parrot's head and neck.

Zoe reached out and touched Pearl. Then she looked at them with the biggest smile. That smile made Maddie's day.

Pearl ducked her head down for more.

"She likes that." Maddie watched Zoe closely, loving the respectful way she approached the parrot.

"Hi, Pearl," Zoe cooed.

"Helllloooo."

"Oh, wow. Pearl sounds like Mrs. Doubtfire." Melanie chuckled.

"You're right." Maddie laughed too. She encouraged Dora, but the youngest was a little timid around Pearl. "That's okay, honey. Does Aunt Melanie want to give it a try?"

"Yes, please." Jackson's sister petted Pearl's head and scratched near her neck. "She's really cool. How long have you had her?"

"I grew up with her, but inherited her from my grandfather about five years ago." Maddie had flown home to pick the parrot up while Stan was deployed overseas. Surprisingly, he'd been okay with it because his friends had thought Pearl pretty cool. He did too, at first.

Melanie looked at her. "How old is she?"

Shaking off memories, Maddie answered, "Thirty."

"Thirty?" Melanie asked. "I didn't realize they lived that long."

"Some species can live up to seventy years," Maddie answered. She placed Pearl on the back of the wooden high chair. "My grandfather got her as a baby before he retired from the Marines."

"Is that her high chair?" Melanie laughed.

"Yup." Maddie went to the fridge and grabbed a cup of Pearl's chopped fruit and veggies, which she placed on the tray.

Zoe stood near the high chair, watching Pearl's every move. "Can I pet her while she's eating?"

"You may. Again, be gentle." Maddie offered Melanie a seat at the kitchen table. Dora climbed into her aunt's lap. "I have iced tea and apple juice."

"Thank you. I think I will take some iced tea. The girls might like juice."

"Yeah!" Dora leaned back against her aunt.

Maddie kept an eye on Zoe with Pearl as she gathered the drinks and set them on the table. "Zoe, you are really good with Pearl."

"Thank you." Zoe was ear-to-ear smiles. "Will she talk to me?"

"After she eats, she might if you tell her she's a pretty bird." Maddie slipped into a chair facing Melanie. "I was about her age when my grandfather moved in with me and my mom and brought Pearl."

"Did you grow up in Pine?"

"I did. How about you?"

"Escanaba. I'm staying here till Friday to watch the girls while Jackson gets settled into his new job."

"That's nice of you. I noticed your wedding ring. Your husband doesn't mind?" Maddie had to account for every detail of her day when Stan was home.

Melanie shrugged. "He knows Jackson's been through a lot. So tell me, what kind of jobs are you looking for?"

Maddie's heart pinched at that simple statement. She could only imagine what Jackson had gone through after his wife's overdose. Curious to know more, she figured now wasn't the time or place to ask questions. Especially with the girls hanging on their words. So, she explained her sewing aspirations, which resulted in a tour of her craft room and the clothing she'd made.

"Did you make what you're wearing?" Melanie asked.

"I did." Maddie's designs were simple and comfortable. They went well with the soft fabrics she used, like superfine corduroy, linen and cotton. She'd been told they were too unconstructed and boxy, but Maddie liked a less-fitted style. Fashion trends came and went, but Maddie thought her designs were sort of classic. She wore them all the time.

"That's amazing. Do you sell them?" Melanie walked

over to one of the many perches on top of a splat mat Maddie had placed throughout her two-bedroom home. This perch happened to have a bird rope hanging from the ceiling right next to it. "For Pearl?"

Maddie laughed. "She keeps me company when I'm working. I tried selling them online, but with the shipping and then the returns, it was more headache than pleasure. Come on. Let's go into the living room, where it's more comfortable."

"Can Pearl come too?" Zoe asked.

"Of course." Maddie fetched Pearl from the kitchen, where she made her usual clicking noises to announce she was done with her food. She placed the parrot on top of her cage. "She might go in and play with her toys."

"She has a lot of toys," Zoe said with a giggle. "You're a pretty bird."

"Pretty bird, pretty." Pearl followed up with a screech and whistle.

Dora covered her ears and giggled.

Maddie laughed too.

"Hello, Pearl." Zoe looked like she loved every minute of the parrot's attention.

"Hellloooo."

Both girls were easy to be around, and Maddie wished to give them as much joy as she could. The fact that they were so well-behaved after losing their mother spoke volumes about Jackson's care. Or maybe they were on their best behavior because of their aunt. Whatever it was, Maddie was glad they were here.

Zoe kept talking to Pearl and Dora drew closer to the parrot cage while Maddie chatted easily with Melanie. A knock on the door surprised her.

Maddie glanced at the clock as she stood. It was nearly six. "Who—"

"Probably Jackson wondering where we are." Melanie made a face.

Maddie opened the door and her pulse kicked up a notch at the sight of him. Jackson's hair glistened with rain and the royal blue rain jacket he wore made his eyes even brighter. Yep, he was a surefire Romeo come to life. "Hi. Come in. They're here."

"Thanks." He stepped inside.

"Can I take your coat?"

"I just came for the girls…" His gaze strayed to where Zoe stood petting Pearl. Alarmed, he asked, "Is that okay?"

Maddie grinned. "Of course. Zoe is great with her. Give me your coat. It's soaked."

He handed it over but never took his eyes off his daughters.

"Daddy!" Zoe flew toward her father.

Dora too.

Maddie glanced at Pearl. The parrot wasn't the least bit bothered by the commotion or noise. She merely preened her feathers.

Jackson bent down in time to hug both girls. "Having fun?"

"Yes," Dora said.

"Pearl talked to me." Zoe pulled her father by the hand toward the parrot cage.

"Hang on, Zoe. We've got to get home and fix dinner." Jackson still looked wary when it came to Pearl.

Melanie stood. "Dinner is in the Crock-Pot, but I should head over there and check on it." Then she gave Jackson two thumbs up. "Come on, girls. Let's get dinner on the table."

"But I want to stay with Pearl." Zoe folded her arms and frowned.

"You can come see her again, Zoe. As long as it's all right with your dad," Maddie offered.

"Can I?" Zoe's big brown eyes pleaded.

"We'll see."

"Yay!" Zoe jumped up and down. Evidently, *we'll see* translated to *yes* in this little girl's point of view.

Melanie helped Dora into her coat. "Come on, Zoe. I could really use your help."

Zoe gave Pearl a final pet and then dashed toward her aunt. "'Bye."

"'Bye, 'bye." Pearl followed up with a click and whistle.

"I'll be over in a minute. I'd like to ask Maddie something." Jackson stayed put.

Maddie ignored the breathless feeling that took hold of her. She glanced at his sister, who smiled as if she knew what this was about. Surely, he wasn't going to ask her out?

When the door closed, Jackson turned to her. "Thank you for having them."

"Of course."

Running his hand through damp hair, Jackson shifted, looking uneasy. "I was wondering if you'd consider watching Dora after preschool until the daycare has room for her. It could be as long as the first of the year."

Maddie realized what Melanie's thumbs-up signal was for. This wasn't about a date. "So that's why your sister came over."

Jackson looked sheepish. "I meant no offense, but I wanted to get her opinion before I asked you. Besides, they were all itching to meet Pearl."

"No offense taken." Maddie couldn't be offended when Melanie had been genuinely kind and friendly. "Why don't we sit down?"

"Hellloooo," Pearl squawked.

Jackson cringed. "How much does she say?"

"She knows a few words and phrases. You can pet her, if you'd like to."

Jackson carefully sat on the couch, eyeing the parrot. "I don't know."

"Come, Pearl." Maddie lifted her hand and laughed as Jackson ducked when Pearl flew toward her. Served him right for putting his sister up to checking her out. "There, see? Harmless."

"She won't bite?"

"She shouldn't." Pearl had only bitten Stan. Maddie stroked Pearl's feathers and sat down near the middle of the couch. "Go ahead."

Jackson reached out his hand, then pulled it back. "I don't know."

"Zoe had no trouble at all. Dora was a little shy with her."

"Dora's smart." Jackson tentatively reached out again. Pearl hopped right onto Jackson's finger. "Who's nice?"

"Ahhh." Jackson looked really nervous.

Maddie chuckled. "Don't worry. She likes you or she wouldn't have jumped onto your hand."

"Great."

Pearl dipped her head toward him. "Kisses?"

Now Jackson laughed. "Does she know what she's saying?"

Maddie reached for Pearl. She hopped onto Maddie's hand, so she kissed her beak. "I think so. Some, anyway. Other words are just mimicked sounds. Here, now you can touch her."

Jackson gently stroked the back of her head. "She's soft."

Pearl clicked and leaned in for more pets.

"Yes." Maddie was encouraged by the interaction.

If Pearl truly liked Jackson, that was a good sign. Her grandfather had been a gentle man, and Pearl seemed to sense the difference between kindness and cruelty in others. Pearl had never liked Stan.

"I'll put her in her cage so we can talk."

Jackson let out his breath as if relieved. "Okay."

"Who's nice?" Pearl repeated.

"You are, Pearl. You're a pretty bird." Maddie placed the parrot into her cage.

"That's a huge setup," Jackson said.

"Parrots need room to move and play." She chuckled when Pearl rang her bell as if proving her point.

Jackson watched Pearl for a bit, then turned toward Maddie. "Back to my question. Maddie, I want to be frank. I'll pay you the same rate the daycare charges." He handed over the price list from Pine Daycare.

Maddie glanced at the generous amount, then back at Jackson. "That's more than fair."

"You'll need to pick Dora up from preschool, and on days when I have to stay after school for band rehearsal, I'd like you to get Zoe too. It looks like that will be Tuesdays and Thursdays, but if something changes, I'll give you plenty of notice."

Maddie considered both doable.

Another rake through his damp hair. "Also, with your verbal permission—" his bright blue eyes never wavered from hers "—I'd like to run a background check."

Maddie thought about his offer. She didn't mind a background check; she had nothing to hide and she understood Jackson's desire to get one. The payment was more than enough. The girls were great and she'd probably enjoy spending time with them. Pearl would too.

The biggest drawback was the man offering her the job. She found Jackson attractive—she thought of him as Romeo. Would that interfere with working for him? Not if she didn't let it. Besides, when he came home, she'd leave. Simple.

"Think it over and let me know." Jackson got up and pulled his cell phone out of his back pocket. "Can we exchange numbers?"

"Yes." Maddie stood too, rattling off her phone number. She'd been looking for something to fill her time. "I'll do it. In fact, I look forward to it. Zoe and Dora are wonderful girls. You've done a good job by them."

Jackson gazed at her as if trying to see through her. Finally, he spoke. "Thank you. If you can come over this week, Melanie will show you the ropes."

Maddie nodded. "Great."

"Thank you. This will really help me out." Jackson smiled and it lit up his face and crinkled the lines around his eyes.

"Me too," Maddie agreed. Something productive to fill her days besides sewing jumpsuits and overalls.

"We'll talk again this week." Jackson headed toward the door.

Maddie followed. "Jackson?"

He turned. "Yes?"

"Thanks for letting the girls meet Pearl. Zoe is really good with her and, well, your daughter just beamed."

Jackson looked beyond her to Pearl's cage as he shrugged into his jacket. "You were right. She's a gentle bird."

"Thank you." Maddie should point out that Pearl responded well to people who were gentle with her, but didn't. Instead, she held the door for him and grimaced at the driving rain outside. "Yikes. It's really coming down. Good night."

"Night, Maddie." He slipped outside and dashed across their side-by-side driveways.

She watched him the whole way before finally shutting her door. Leaning against it, Maddie smiled at finding a job that promised to keep her busy.

Even if it was only temporary, she'd enjoy these next couple of months or more. She'd keep a wise distance when it came to Romeo, but that might be more difficult with his daughters. If Maddie wasn't careful, she'd fall in love with those girls and wish they were hers.

# *Chapter Four*

"Maddie, would you like to stay for dinner? Jackson is bringing home pizza." Melanie straightened the last framed photograph of Jackson's family on the dining room wall. Right over a baby grand piano.

A dark-eyed beauty who must have been his late wife stared out from the matte finish. From the looks of the girls' individual portraits that hung on either side of the family photo, these were taken a while ago, when Dora was only a toddler.

Zoe resembled her mother, while Dora looked more like her father.

"I should probably go."

"Why? Do you have other plans?" Jackson's sister wiggled her eyebrows.

"No." Maddie laughed, but seeing these personal photographs made her nervous, like she'd been eaves-dropping and was about to get caught.

"Then stay. It's my last evening, and Jackson will prob-ably want to talk to you about taking the reins tomorrow anyway."

That was probably true. She'd gotten a text from him this morning that her background check came back clear.

So, tomorrow she'd be on her own with the girls since Melanie was anxious to get back to her home and husband.

Letting out a breath, Maddie gave in. "Okay."

"Good. I mean, it's pizza, right? Gotta stay for that."

"I suppose so." Maddie had been hanging out with Melanie these last couple of days.

They'd gone over the girls' routines and school schedules, and today, she'd helped Melanie hang some curtains. Now Maddie watched as Melanie finished putting up artwork and photos on the walls downstairs. Jackson's sister had a good eye for the placement of things.

"She was really beautiful," Maddie whispered.

Melanie stood back and stared at the grouping of those three frames. "Delia was that. She'd swept Jackson off his feet like some beautiful hurricane, but he's still cleaning up the mess."

"Hmm." Maddie wondered what she meant by that and was about to ask when Dora ran into the room. The questions teetering on the tip of her tongue stayed there.

"I'm hungry." The four-year-old looked up at those photos and stuck her fingers in her mouth.

Maddie felt a sharp pinch to her heart.

"We're eating soon. Your dad is bringing home pizza."

"Yay!" From sadness to elation, Dora switched gears fast.

"Can I set the table or make a salad or something?" Maddie offered.

"If you'd make a salad, that'd be great. I'll run upstairs and gather my stuff."

"Can I go with you, Aunt Mel?" Zoe hovered against the entrance to the dining room. She noticed the pictures as well and her dark eyes looked somber.

"Come on." Melanie held out her hand for Zoe to take, then glanced back. "Thanks, Maddie."

"Sure thing." Maddie headed for the kitchen. "Dora, do you want to help me?"

"Okay."

Maddie opened the fridge and peered at the shelves packed with different items from what she usually bought. Flavored yogurts and juice boxes stared back at her. *Way too much sugar.* Maddie gathered up salad fixings with both hands when she felt a tug on her sweater.

"Uppy?" Dora reached up.

Maddie chuckled. "My hands are full, sweetie. How about I set these down and then get you a chair to stand on?"

"Yeah."

"Yes?" Maddie automatically corrected.

"Yes."

Maddie pulled a chair from the kitchen table and rested it backward against the sink. "Come on up and we can wash our hands."

Dora climbed onto the chair and then stood while Maddie turned on the water and gave a generous squirt of liquid hand soap into little hands.

Peering out the window over the deep porcelain sink, Maddie had a clear view into her own kitchen window, the one positioned over her sink. Funny that she and Jackson hadn't spotted each other before. Great, she was going to look for him every time she loaded her dishwasher.

*Juliet searching for Romeo.*

Dora grinned up at her. "Now what?"

Maddie shook off that thought and tapped the end of the girl's nose. "Now we wash the lettuce and veggies and make a salad."

Dora made a face. "I don't like *salwed*."

"You don't?" Maddie smiled at her pronunciation. "Why not?"

Dora shrugged. "I dunno."

"Maybe we can find out." Maddie looked in the cupboards until she found a salad bowl. It didn't appear that Jackson owned a spinner, so they'd have to wash and dry the lettuce by hand. She pulled out another bowl, placed it in the sink and filled it with cold water. Then she layered paper towels on the counter.

"I have the perfect job for you, Dora. Can you tear these leaves into that bowl of water?"

The four-year-old nodded and got busy tearing. Her brow furrowed as she concentrated on the task.

And Maddie's heart melted—completely and forever captured by one four-year-old. *Uh-oh*.

"Here, we don't have to make them really small." Maddie tore the lettuce in larger pieces. "Like this."

Dora worked even harder, her expression serious.

"That's it. Good job." Maddie rinsed the other veggies and started slicing them into the salad bowl.

She was going to like watching the Taylor girls. She could relate to the heartache of losing a loved one. Even after five years, it still hurt when she thought of her grandfather dying from cancer at only sixty-eight.

It wasn't just losing their mother that made Maddie want to give these two little girls as much joy as she could. They seemed wounded as well, beaten down by something they didn't even understand. Maddie knew about those feelings too. She'd never grasp why Stan had treated her the way he did, loving one moment, then downright mean and menacing the next.

She spotted Jackson's car pulling into the driveway and her heart raced.

*Really.* Was she still a teenager or what?

She watched as he got out of the car and then grabbed two huge pizza boxes from the passenger seat. She would like a relationship someday with the right man. The challenge was knowing who could be a *right man*. She'd made such a huge mistake the first time around, she didn't trust herself not to make that same mistake again.

She heard the side porch door open and briefly closed her eyes. Go time. She could handle this attraction if she could just ignore it.

"Hey, Mel—" Jackson stopped. "You're not Melanie. Hi, Maddie. I hope you're staying for dinner." He lifted the boxes before setting them on the kitchen table. "We have plenty."

"Yes, your sister invited me to stay." She didn't want him to think she'd decided to stick around without being asked.

"Good. We can go over tomorrow and next week's schedule." Jackson jerked on the tie he wore beneath a sweater-vest, loosening it.

She'd been used to men in camo fatigues and T-shirts. The stuffy attire suited Jackson and made him seem more gentlemanly somehow. But then, appearances could be deceiving.

"I'm helping," Dora said.

He narrowed his gaze. "You are? Doing what?"

"Making *salwed.*" The little girl brought her lettuce-filled hands up, dripping water all over.

"Whoa, keep it over the sink there." Jackson swung in for a quick nuzzle against his daughter's cheek.

Dora giggled.

Maddie smiled even though an ache from deep inside her grew and twisted with regret. She'd never had kids of her own. Because of her impulsive decision to elope with Stan, she'd missed out on a lot of good living. She'd grown to hate him for all that too.

Could she make up for lost time with the Taylors? It was a daunting idea no matter how she looked at it and much too soon to act on it.

Jackson tried not to let the image of his pretty neighbor giving Dora the chance to tear lettuce get to him. His wife used to let the girls help in the kitchen, and those echoes of sweet laughter rang through his mind. There had been good times along with the bad.

"I'm going to go change." He needed to get out of that kitchen.

When he'd swooped in to kiss his daughter, he'd caught a whiff of Maddie's soft perfume. It was a subtle scent, sweet and flowery. Nice. He was far too tempted to capture another sniff, so he'd backed away quickly.

"Would you like me to put the pizza in the oven to keep warm?" Maddie asked.

"Sure." He didn't care about the temperature of pizza. Neither did his girls, but whatever.

Dashing upstairs, he overheard Zoe and his sister chatting about Zoe's new school. Zoe liked her second-grade teacher and had already made friends. Talk about a huge relief.

He peeked into the guest bedroom where Mel had been staying. "Ready to head home?"

His sister looked up and smiled. "I am."

Zoe ran for him. "Daddy!"

He scooped her up. "How was your day?"

Zoe proceeded to tell him everything that had happened at school. "And then Maddie and Aunt Mel picked me up and we got ice cream."

"Wow!" He glanced at his sister.

She shrugged. "It was Maddie's idea."

"Really?" So, Maddie liked ice cream. He'd have to remember that. "Why don't you go get washed up for dinner?"

He let his daughter down and she dashed off to the bathroom. He focused on his sister. "How'd it go today? Is she ready to take over?"

Mel waved her hand as if Maddie watching the girls was a no-brainer. "She's really good with them. I mean, really good. So, yeah, she's ready."

"Good." That was a huge load off his shoulders. "I can't thank you enough for staying this week."

"You're my brother—of course I'd stay. Do you want to know what else?" His sister cocked her head as if she was about to share a big secret.

Jackson narrowed his gaze. "What?"

"I think she'd be good for you too."

Jackson backed up a few steps. "Not happening."

His sister stepped toward him. "I know it's only been a year, but just keep an open mind, you know, for the future."

"No, Mel. I'm done with all that." He meant it too, but then, why'd he notice every little thing about his pretty neighbor? "I've got to change. Leave your bag, and I'll take it downstairs."

His sister shook her head. "I got it."

Jackson escaped to his room to change out of his work clothes. Slipping into a pair of jeans and a sweatshirt, he could hear voices from downstairs wafting up through the heat register. He could detect Maddie and Zoe and Dora, along with the occasional clink of silverware. They were setting the table. He couldn't make out their words, only murmurs and laughter. The sound of his girls' giggles always soothed, reassuring him that they still found joy in day-to-day things.

He exited his room and bounded down the stairs. Melanie was in the kitchen along with Maddie and the girls when he walked in. The tantalizing aroma of pepperoni pizza made his mouth water. He spotted the boxes on the table along with a bowl of salad and bottled dressings.

He glanced at Maddie, who took charge of opening the cheese pizza box to serve the girls like she'd done it a thousand times.

"We already prayed, Daddy." Zoe held up her plate.

Maddie regarded him as if worried that might upset him. "I hope you don't mind."

"Not at all." A sliver of guilt pricked his conscience. Leading the dinnertime prayer used to be his job, until he quit. He sat down at the table and reached for a steaming slice of pepperoni pizza. "Thanks for the salad."

"I helped," Dora chimed in.

"I know you did. Are you going to eat some?" Jackson filled a bowl with salad greens and then squirted Italian dressing on top.

Dora shook her head.

Jackson held out a forkful. "Just a bite."

Again, she shook her head.

Maddie grabbed the ranch dressing and made a little glob of it on her plate. Then she dipped a single slice of cucumber into the ranch before eating it. And repeated the same thing with a clump of lettuce. He'd never seen anyone eat salad ingredients one at a time.

Dora watched her too, and then pointed. "Can I try?"

Jackson exchanged a surprised look with his sister. It was not easy getting his youngest to eat vegetables. Then he looked at his neighbor. "Who are you, Madelyn Williams?"

Maddie muffled a laugh and shrugged as she dipped a tomato wedge into her pool of ranch.

Melanie served up the salad for Dora along with ranch dressing, and sure enough, Dora dug right in. One veggie at a time.

Jackson heard his sister's comment about Maddie being good with the girls run through his thoughts. Getting Dora to eat raw veggies was a huge win. It appeared that Maddie might be just what the girls needed as Melanie went back to her world.

He didn't want to think about his needs.

It was funny that the fascination with their neighbor had started out with a big gray parrot he'd been afraid to touch. Maddie was definitely different from the women he'd known, but similar in the one way that mattered most—she was way too attractive. Regardless of Mel's belief that she'd be good for him, Jackson knew that he could mess up this seemingly perfect situation if he didn't keep a cautious distance.

Dinner was great, and Maddie was sorry to see it come to an end. She was sorry to see Melanie leave as well. She felt as if she'd made a friend there. As Melanie gave hugs to each of her nieces, Maddie busied herself with clearing the table. Jackson had wanted to go over the upcoming schedules, so she couldn't leave yet. As nerve-racking as it was to be around him, she found that she didn't relish leaving, either. Only Pearl waited for her at home.

"'Bye, Maddie. Call me if you need anything or just want to talk."

"I will." Maddie returned the quick hug. "Thanks."

"Maddie, leave the dishes. I can do them later." Jackson walked his sister out to her car, carrying both her suitcase and laptop.

The girls had gone into the living room and clicked on the TV.

She could hear the sound of cartoons, and then Zoe asked Dora if she wanted to watch *Bugs Bunny* or something else.

Maddie chuckled. Zoe was a good big sister, always looking out for Dora. Maddie had been an only child, growing up without a father, but a grandfather and his parrot had taken that place. Maddie's grandmother had passed away when she was a baby.

She scanned the counter. She wasn't about to leave dishes that could easily be loaded into the dishwasher while she waited for Jackson's return. It didn't take long.

"Thanks, but you didn't have to do that," Jackson said as he entered the kitchen. The wind had messed with his short dark hair, causing a thick fringe to lie across his forehead.

She clasped her hands to keep from smoothing his hair back. "No big deal. So, you wanted to go over tomorrow and next week."

"Yes. Zoe has only half a day tomorrow due to teacher conferences, so do you mind picking her up after you get Dora? I'll be home by four."

"No problem." Melanie had already given her a heads-up, asking if she'd mind watching Zoe as well as Dora on her first official day as their after-school caregiver.

"And then next week, it'll be regular schedule. I have band rehearsals after school on Tuesdays and Thursdays."

"Got it."

Jackson ran his hand through his hair, somewhat fixing what the wind had done. "Thank you for doing all this."

"You're paying me well, remember?" Maddie wanted to reestablish their working relationship. He was her employer. It'd be best to keep that front and center. Especially in her mind. "The least I can do is clean up after dinner."

Jackson chuckled. "Right. Anyway, I'm still glad you agreed to watch the girls. Now leave the rest for me, okay?"

Maddie smiled and hung the dishcloth over the edge of the sink. The only thing left was wiping off the table. "Okay. I'll head home."

"I'll walk you out."

Maddie felt the annoying zip of nerves and squashed them. She followed him toward the side entrance that opened into a mudroom of sorts between the dining room and living room. The side porch that faced her house ran the length of the dining room that was off the kitchen.

She stopped in the middle of the space. "Jackson, would you be okay with the girls coming to my house tomorrow afternoon?"

He considered it and nodded. "Sure. They'd probably love seeing Pearl."

"That's what I thought too." Maddie grabbed her jacket from the large wooden hall tree against the wall. It had a bench with shelves below it where the girls stashed their shoes.

"They're messy," he warned.

Maddie chuckled. "And a parrot isn't?"

"I see your point."

"Well, good night, then." She really didn't want to leave, which was silly. Scary too.

"Good night, Maddie."

She ducked out the door into chilly evening air. The temperature had definitely dropped since the sun had set. She wouldn't be surprised to see frost come morning.

Maddie darted across their driveways and made it quickly to her front door. "Pearl, I'm home."

"Hellloooo."

She stepped into her living room and unlatched Pearl's cage to let her fly free. The parrot headed straight for the kitchen, probably wanting a snack. Maddie made the short way there, and sure enough, Pearl was perched on the back of her high chair.

Maddie had filled up Pearl's pellet dish before she'd gone next door, but Pearl was looking for something fresher. Maddie grabbed a banana and some walnuts. She chopped a small portion in a dish and placed it on the high chair's tray.

Pearl whistled and then dug in, sending bits of banana and nuts flying.

Maddie scratched her parrot's neck, then headed for the kitchen sink to wash her hands. Peering through the window, she spotted Jackson at his kitchen sink. The soft glow of recessed lighting from above him made him look like he was onstage. He did have a noble air about him. All Jackson needed was a puffy purple doublet and he'd nail Romeo for sure.

She sighed and stepped away from the window. She really shouldn't cast herself as Juliet. Not only was there too much tragedy in that romantic tale, but she'd failed miserably in her first relationship. Even though Jackson might prove to be very different from Stan, her immediate attraction to him was very similar to how she'd felt toward her late husband before they'd eloped.

Stan had been outgoing, handsome and athletic. He'd pursued her with compliments until her head had spun. The first couple of years with Stan had been pretty good. Sure, he'd been a little overbearing perhaps, wanting to know where she was and with whom practically every minute of every day. At first, she'd written off his over-protectiveness as sort of romantic. But it gradually escalated to jealous rages and bouts of anger over the least little thing.

Jackson had a protective streak when it came to his girls, but that was probably different. Still, she'd been fooled once, and there was no way she'd allow herself to be fooled again. Any man could turn cruel given the right circumstances, couldn't they? They probably could. She was better off on her own, with no one to answer to but herself.

Maddie looked around her kitchen with its oak cupboards and oak table. She didn't have a lot of knickknacks to display, and she hadn't wanted any pictures that might remind her of Stan. Even the soft yellow valances she'd made for the windows seemed boring. She needed to add color in her house. Her clothes too. She'd played it safe and surrounded herself with nothing that might be considered risky. It didn't make her feel any better. It felt lonely and bland.

Her phone buzzed, startling her. It was her mom. "Hello?"

"How's my girl?"

Maddie laughed. "Fine. Actually, I start a new job tomorrow."

"You do? Doing what?"

"I'm going to watch my neighbor's two little girls after school."

"Maddie, that's wonderful. Good for you."

"I think so too. At least for now. The job is only temporary for the next couple of months or so. What's up?"

"Paul and I want to have you over for dinner Sunday. Are you busy?"

"No. That should work."

"Perfect. Come right after your church service."

"Will do." Maddie's mind wandered when her mom

explained what they were having for dinner, complete with Paul's supposedly famous chocolate-chip brownies.

It wasn't that she didn't like her stepfather; she just didn't know him. When she'd made the trip to look at houses after Stan died, Maddie had stayed with her mom, and Paul had been away for some reason during that time.

Her mother had remarried almost two years ago, while Maddie lived in North Carolina. She'd driven the whole long way to attend the wedding so she could bring Pearl while Stan had been deployed. Weddings were not the place to get to know the groom, but Maddie's first impression hadn't been good. He reminded her too much of Stan.

Paul was her mother's world now. She seemed happy too, but that could be a facade. Maddie had been good at hiding the darker parts of her life. She might not be as close to her mother as she should be, but they were alike in so many ways. Bad taste in men being front and center.

After ending the call, Maddie cleaned up after Pearl. As she rinsed the flat dish in the sink, she peered out her window to the house next door, but the Taylor kitchen was dark. What were they up to?

She listened closely and heard the hammering of keys on the piano, which made her smile. No doubt Zoe's piano lessons were in progress. The last couple of afternoons spent with Zoe and Dora had been noisy but fun.

The silence in her house seemed deafening, and Maddie wished she were with Jackson and his girls.

# Chapter Five

Jackson scarfed his sandwich in the half hour he had between his morning music classes and afternoon instrument lessons or band instruction at the connected high school. Tuesdays and Thursdays were band days, both afternoon instruction and after-school rehearsals. Monday and Wednesday afternoons were middle-school music lessons—individual and group. Friday afternoons he gave lessons at the high school.

His phone dinged with an incoming text. He saw that it came from Maddie and his heart stopped. Fearing the worst, but hoping everything was okay, he opened the message.

Hi Jackson. Just picked up Zoe. I have both girls and we're headed for my house.

He texted back his thanks and breathed a little easier. Day one and no issues.

The girls had been so excited about Maddie picking them up today. He'd had a hard time getting them out the door this morning. Zoe wouldn't stand still for him to braid her hair, so he'd drawn her dark locks into a ponytail. Dora too. She followed her sister's lead. Question after question, his oldest had grilled him—would Maddie take them for ice cream? Would they go see Pearl? It had been all he could do to get them bundled up in their coats and leaving on time.

Their excitement had been a nice confirmation that he'd made the right choice. His sister leaving the two car seats that she used for the girls had been a huge help as well. Maddie put them in the back seat of her car, where they'd stay until no longer needed. This arrangement had every indication of working perfectly. As long as nothing went wrong.

He took the last bite of his ham-and-Swiss and then guzzled the rest of his pop. He looked around his little corner of the music room. Nothing other than the picture of his girls belonged to him. The music books had all come from previous teachers and the modest selection of instruments had been supplied by the school. Rural schools definitely had less money to allocate for the arts, but Pine Public Schools did the best they could. He'd eventually go through everything, but not now.

Jackson grabbed his coat and satchel, and headed for the band room in the high school. It didn't take long to walk there through the connecting hallway that had been warmed by the sun beating in through the large windows. He knew it was cold outside, though. The temps had been frigid this morning, but no snow.

Once in the band room where he gave lessons and the band learned new material, he set his stuff on the chair and scanned the large area. Chairs with music stands had been set up in a semicircle around a small podium. The instruments were old but functional. Some kids had their own and kept them in the line of lockers along the far wall during the day.

Between the upcoming Veterans Day Program and the Christmas concert, they had a lot of music to cover. A lot of improvement needed to be accomplished, which justified the after-school rehearsals on Tuesdays and Thursdays. He glanced at the clock. He had time before his lesson started, so he approached the line of bookcases under the windows. He hadn't really looked at what was housed there and hunched down to get a better view. Yearbooks from antiquity to current day were lined up by year. Interesting.

He pulled a random yearbook from about eight years ago and leafed through it. There was a small section specific to band with pictures of concerts and classes littering two pages. He found himself smiling at some of the sillier shots of students. He'd been a band geek back in his high school and had loved every minute.

Those experiences, coupled with an instructor who'd encouraged him, made Jackson want to be a music teacher. There was something special about that transition of simply reading notes on a page to actually feeling the music. Seeing that connection never got old, and guiding students through the process made the job more than worth it.

Flipping through the pages, he spotted a picture of a cheerleader who looked a lot like Maddie. And yet not. This young beauty didn't wear glasses but did wear a whole lot of makeup. He turned to the section of class pictures and went to the senior pages. He tried to remember Maddie's maiden name that he'd seen listed in her background check—Heath. Madelyn Heath.

He found her in the middle of the *H*s, and sure enough, a younger, seemingly more confident version of his neighbor stared out at him from the glossy page. It wasn't just the lack of glasses that made this Maddie seem so different. It was the expectant smile, as if she couldn't wait to see what life ahead held. The Maddie he knew seemed to hide. His first glimpse of her, she'd ducked out of sight.

He turned the pages toward the end of the alphabet and scanned the seniors with the last name of Williams. There were only two. Jennifer and Stan. And Stan looked like a typical jock—big and burly. Surely, he wasn't Maddie's dead husband.

"Hey, Mr. Taylor." One of his band students had arrived for clarinet lessons. The kid was also interested in conducting.

"Hi, Tom." Jackson closed the yearbook with a snap. Back to work.

But that wide-eyed version of Maddie pestered his thoughts the rest of the day. Something or someone had changed her. It was only a senior picture, but still, the differences he'd seen didn't sit well with him. Not at all.

"Come on, girls. Let's head over to your house." Maddie placed Pearl back in her cage.

"I like your house." Zoe stood near Pearl's cage.

"You do? How come?" Maddie glanced at Dora lying on her belly on the couch. She had her two fingers in her mouth as she'd watched her sister interact with the parrot.

Dora still kept her distance from Pearl. Her big blue eyes took in every detail, though, not missing a thing. She looked just like her father—observing and cautious.

Zoe shrugged. "Pearl's here."

Pearl rang her bell.

"Well, I like your house too." Maddie smiled. She loved it, actually, with the expansive rooms and big, white kitchen. It felt like a home, while her house was just a place to live. "Come on. Let's get into coats, mittens and hats."

"'Bye, Pearl." Zoe waved toward the cage.

"'Bye, 'bye," Pearl said and then whistled.

It didn't take long to get bundled up against the cold wind that blew out of the north, chilling Maddie to her core. Stepping outside, she sank deeper into her down coat and wished she'd grabbed a hat.

She reached her glove-covered hands out to each girl and held tight. "Let's run."

They all giggled as they ran across two driveways while the wind tore at their hair and clothes. Maddie used her key, the one Melanie had given her, to open the side porch door. They entered and the girls slipped out of their coats and dropped them on the floor while they ripped off hats and mittens and stuffed them into a basket at the base of the hall tree.

"Race ya!" Zoe ran for the living room.

Dora followed her sister, her chubby little legs wrapped in flowered leggings pumping hard to keep up. She was the cutest thing.

"Whoa, girls, you forgot to hang up your coats." Too late, they were gone. Maddie scooped them up and hung them next to hers. She rubbed her arms. "Brrrr, it's cold in here."

She tended to keep the thermostat in her house higher than the recommended sixty-eight degrees—not only for herself, but for Pearl. Still, her house was much smaller than this one. Maddie stepped into the living room and considered the brick fireplace and hearth that took up nearly the whole wall.

The charred remains of a log lay in the grate behind a fire screen decorated with scrolling filigree. A hefty amount of wood was stacked in a cast-iron holder on the brick hearth.

Maddie pointed at the fireplace. "Zoe, do you have fires often?"

The little girl nodded and clicked on the TV. "Daddy builds them."

That was enough for Maddie. She hoped Jackson didn't mind, but it was either that or turn up the heat. People could be funny about their thermostats, so she didn't want to mess with it. Her mother had always been finicky about turning up the heat. Since she'd be hanging out for the next hour in the living room with the girls until Jackson got home around four, a cozy little fire might be welcomed. At least, she hoped so.

Maddie moved the screen, then stacked some kindling on the charred piece and placed a small log on top. Using a long match from a box on the mantel, Maddie struck it. For a moment she hesitated, wondering how Jackson might react. Stan would come unglued at the least little thing she did wrong and then apologize profusely afterward, but the damage had always been done.

Maddie felt the heat of the flame inching toward her fingers and made her decision. If Jackson didn't want her starting fires, he should have said something. She held the nearly burnt match under the kindling until flames licked the wood and then dropped it on top. The crackling sound of fire spreading over dry tinder soothed far more than the silly cartoons that blared in the background.

Maddie spotted a bookshelf with several games and children's books stacked amid an interesting array of both nonfiction and fiction. She'd scope out those books another time. "Girls, would you rather play a game instead of watching TV?"

"Yeah," Dora said. She had grabbed a knitted throw blanket and was curled into it.

Zoe tipped her head. "What game?"

"You choose."

Zoe went to the bookshelf, ran her fingers over the boxes and chose *Candyland*. "How about this one?"

"One of my favorites." Maddie clicked off the TV, threw another couple of logs on the fire and then sat down on the huge overstuffed couch she'd seen the movers hauling out of the truck that first day.

Zoe handed her the box, then settled in next to her. Dora scooted close as well. The girls must be chilled too. Feeling the warmth of the fire wash over her like a hot North Carolina breeze, Maddie finally thawed. She'd deal with Jackson's reaction when the time came. For now, she'd enjoy the heat.

She opened the box and sorted out the game cards and plastic gingerbread movers. "What color would you like to be?"

"Green," Zoe called out.

"Boo." Dora didn't bother pronouncing the *l*.

"Blue?" Maddie held out the gingerbread piece.

"Yes." Dora reached for it.

Maddie choose yellow and they started the game. In no time, Zoe's gingerbread mover was way ahead. "Look at you go."

Zoe drew a card. "I got the lollipop!" And she jumped even farther ahead.

Maddie chuckled as she drew her card and moved to an orange square. She heard the door open, followed by the sound of keys tossed on the counter. *Jackson.*

Maddie clenched her hands. What would he think of her building a fire?

"Hello." Jackson stepped into the living room. "What are you playing?"

"*Candyland* and I'm winning," Zoe said.

It was Dora's turn, but she ran toward her father, who scooped her up. "Are you having fun with Maddie?"

"Yes."

"I hope it was okay to make a fire." Maddie pushed her glasses up the bridge of her nose.

Jackson looked at her. "That's fine. Sorry it was so cold in here. I forgot to turn up the heat this morning. Feel free to do so if I forget again."

She let loose the breath she'd held. "Oh, okay, no problem."

Jackson watched her a moment longer than necessary before plopping Dora back on the couch. He stepped toward the fire, moved the screen and tossed on another two logs, making the flames roar. "Feels good in here. I love that there's a fireplace in this house."

"It's a nice feature." Maddie should leave now that Jackson was home. But if the truth were told, she didn't want to. Must be the cozy fire or no desire to face that wind outside. It had nothing to do with Jackson's hair that looked charmingly tousled.

"I'm hungry. Can I have another snack?" Zoe stood up.

"Me too," Dora added.

Maddie stood as well, feeling torn between getting snacks for the girls and leaving.

Jackson waved her back down. "Relax. I'll get it."

Maddie watched him leave, with Zoe racing in front of him. Dora remained on the couch with two fingers in her mouth. Maddie really should go—that was the deal she'd made with herself. There was no reason to stick around.

Zoe ran back into the living room. "We're going to make s'mores!"

"That sounds fun." Maddie got up and headed for the kitchen. She should tell Jackson she was leaving. Zoe followed her. So did Dora.

He filled a tray with marshmallows, chocolate bars and graham crackers. "What else do we need?"

"Milk," Dora said.

"Milk it is." Jackson opened the fridge and pulled out the plastic jug. Then he noticed her. "What would you like to drink, Maddie?"

"Oh, no. I can't stay."

"Plans?" Jackson asked.

She shook her head. "No. I just—"

"But we haven't finished our game," Zoe piped up.

"Your dad can take my place." It was far too tempting to stay.

Zoe's face fell. "But that's not fair."

"I could use some help roasting the marshmallows." Jackson's blue eyes pleaded.

Her resolve crumbled like a stale graham cracker. "Do you have roasting sticks?"

He grinned. "In the garage. If you take the tray, and the girls, I'll get the sticks."

What was wrong with her? Her first day on the job and already she was breaking her self-made rule of keeping a safe distance from her handsome employer.

Zoe pulled on the hem of her sweater. "Are you coming?"

Maddie blew out a breath. "You go on in. I'll be there after I fill up Dora's sippy cup. Would you like milk too?"

"Yes, please." Zoe gave her a broad smile, looking very happy indeed, before skipping her way back to the living room.

Maddie supposed sticking around was a small price to pay for that smile.

Jackson returned from the garage with two long roasting forks. He'd invited Maddie to stay after seeing that flash of something very close to fear in her eyes when she'd mentioned building a fire. But then she'd looked away so quickly and pushed her glasses back in place, he wasn't exactly sure what he'd seen.

He'd noticed that she did that a lot—look away and fix her eyeglasses as if trying to hide behind the lenses. What had changed her from the bright-eyed teenager with a confident smile to the woman who hid under eyeglasses, gorgeous long hair and the oversized sweaters she wore? Jackson wanted to know the answer.

Besides, it wasn't a bad idea to get to know Maddie a little better as well. He'd hired her to watch his girls, after all. It wasn't that he needed the company. Not at all.

Entering the toasty living room, Jackson looked forward to s'mores there. "This should be fun."

Maddie had the graham crackers prepped with chunks of chocolate on top, ready for melty marshmallows. Efficient.

He removed the screen once again and knelt in front of the fireplace. He stuck both forks into the flames.

"What about the marshmallows?" Zoe scolded him.

"I'm sterilizing these first."

"Can I roast some?" Zoe reached for a fork.

"Hang on. The ends of those prongs are hot." Jackson turned and reached out his hand. "Maddie, can you toss me a couple marshmallows?"

"Sure." Instead of throwing them, she knelt down next to him with the bag and handed him two. "Here you go."

He took the square confections and their fingers got tangled up. He felt the zing of that contact clear up to his shoulder. He chuckled to cover the awkward awareness. "Sorry. Here, you better take the other fork."

She kept the hot end up high, but he noticed a pretty flush of pink on her cheeks. "Dora, do you want to roast this one? I'll help you."

Dora, sipping milk, nodded.

Maddie motioned for his four-year-old to come closer, and Jackson watched as Dora slipped off the couch and right into Maddie's lap as if she belonged there. It was a sweet sight, but a bitter one too.

Delia had kept her distance from Dora toward the end, and Jackson often wondered if she'd done that so she wouldn't lose her nerve. Jackson had missed those signs. He'd never once considered that his wife might end her life. He was beyond grateful that both girls had been with his parents when he found her.

Keeping an eye on Zoe, he reached for the bag. "Want me to put them on?"

"No. I got it," Maddie said.

Without missing a beat and keeping the hot end far from Dora, Maddie slid two marshmallows onto each prong and then helped Dora hold it near the flames.

"Not too close. We don't want to catch it on fire." Maddie gently twisted the fork, so each side of the double-stacked marshmallows turned a light brown.

"Sure we do. That's what makes it fun." Jackson laughed when Zoe's caught on fire.

Maddie's eyes widened, but she laughed too. "I don't think it's good to encourage your daughters to catch their treats on fire."

Zoe didn't look amused with either of them. She stared with disappointment at the little ball of flame. "Now what?"

"Let it burn and we'll make more." Jackson made sure Zoe didn't swing that roasting stick out of the fireplace until the sticky mess had seared off into the flames.

Jackson glanced at Maddie. Her marshmallows were perfect.

"Want some?" Maddie offered a completed s'more.

"Yes, please." Zoe held out her hands.

Jackson took charge of the roasting fork, plunked on a couple more marshmallows and got to work toasting them higher over the flame. He could make them perfect too.

"There's one for you, Jackson," Maddie offered. "Dora and I can make more."

"I'll wait till these are done." He twirled the fork a little and leaned back against the bottom of the recliner where he could keep his girls in view. And Maddie too.

Zoe and Dora each had marshmallow and chocolate smeared around their mouths. This might wreck their appetite for dinner, but he didn't care. It was Friday night and that meant relaxing the rules a little. Even when it came to their pretty neighbor. Especially when it came to her.

He glanced at Maddie. "What are you doing for dinner?"

Her pretty eyes widened. "Nothing much. Probably soup and maybe a sandwich."

"Would you like to have that over here? Then we can go over how the day went with these two."

"We got to play with Pearl," Zoe told him.

Jackson focused on Zoe. "Did you pet her?"

Zoe nodded as she munched on another bite of her s'more.

"Ahhh, Jackson, you might want to turn your fork." Maddie gave his flaming marshmallows a pointed look.

He drew it out, blew on it, then popped the roasting fork back in for a few more seconds. "Almost done. I like 'em burnt."

When he finally pulled the metal stick back, Maddie had two graham crackers ready with chocolate. She used the tops of two more cracker squares to help slide the marshmallows in place. She was an efficient helper.

*My perfect helpmate?* His sister's words about Maddie being good for him too challenged him. Maybe he shouldn't be so quick to dismiss that thought.

Looking up at her, Jackson prompted, "So, are you up for staying? It's Friday night. There's no sense in you eating alone, unless you'd rather—"

Her gaze snapped to his and he thought he saw a little flame ignite in her eyes before they narrowed. "All right, but let me make the sandwiches."

He might have hit a nerve about her eating alone, but he'd spoken the truth. Although, seeing that fire in her eyes had made her look more like the girl in the senior photo. Whether that was a good sign or bad, he didn't know. But he wouldn't mind finding out.

"Deal." He took a huge bite of s'more.

"Now that we've had our snacks, should we finish the game?" Maddie asked.

"Yup." Zoe walked on her knees over to the coffee table.

Dora had crawled up onto the couch with her sippy cup. Her eyes were drooping.

"I think we're going to lose Dora. I'll take her spot." Jackson polished off the last s'more.

Maddie got up and reached for the tray. "Let me take this to the kitchen."

Jackson, still sitting on the floor, watched her go. He'd been about to tell her to leave the tray in case they made more s'mores later, after dinner. But that wouldn't be a smart idea. He got the feeling his girls were in for an early night to bed. If that happened, sitting near the fireplace with Maddie alone would be far too tempting. Better to leave that cozy idea unspoken.

Maddie returned with a couple of damp paper towels. She moved the sippy cup away and wiped off Dora's hands, then her mouth. Then she tucked the knitted throw over his daughter's legs. "Do you want to finish our game?"

"Nope." Dora grabbed her sippy cup and leaned back.

Maddie handed a fresh damp towel to Zoe. "For your fingers."

Zoe cleaned off her hands and handed it back to Maddie.

Maddie tossed the used paper towels into the fire and repositioned the screen, then looked at him. "Ready to play? Dora was the blue gingerbread man."

"I am." Jackson didn't need to discuss how Maddie's first day went watching his daughters. He could easily see that it went great. Perfect, in fact.

Both girls responded well to Maddie, and she was a natural with them. Why didn't she have kids of her own? Clearly, she'd make a great mom. Another mystery? Jackson was definitely curious. Maddie had a story, but should he really try to get her to tell it? Once he started snooping around in her life, he might not like what he found.

## Chapter Six

Thursday afternoon, Maddie grabbed the laundry from the dryer and tossed it into a basket, then headed for the kitchen table to fold it. The dining room table looked too shiny, and Maddie didn't want to scratch the glossy surface with a laundry basket.

There wasn't much counter space in the closet that housed the washer and dryer. There were, however, bifold doors that could be closed to hide the laundry area, keeping the side entrance space neat and tidy.

It had been nearly a week since she'd started taking care of Dora. She watched Zoe only on the two days Jackson stayed after school for band rehearsal. Today had been one of those days, and it was fun having both girls for the afternoon into evening. They'd visited Pearl and were back at their house for a quick snack and finishing laundry.

Maddie set the basket on the kitchen table. Both girls were still munching on a couple of thin slices of apple. "All done?"

"Almost." Zoe still had a chunk to eat.

Dora too.

Maddie folded the girls' clean jeans, leggings and tops

while still warm from the dryer. Her week had flown by and her thoughts had been occupied with how to entertain Zoe and Dora. It was great to have something else to think about instead of obsessing over guilt and bitterness toward her late husband.

She'd met Ruth and Erica for lunch earlier than normal to accommodate her schedule in picking up Dora. Her fellow widows had been congratulatory on her temporary job of watching the girls, but Erica had seemed even more pleased than Ruth.

Erica had a way of hearing more than was said and seeing more than what Maddie revealed. Her excitement over the girls and their dad moving in next door translated into questions about romantic interest, which Maddie denied. She wasn't about to admit that Jackson was her secret Romeo.

Maddie reined in her thoughts and focused on the task of folding clothes. "Oh, no."

"What's wrong?" Zoe asked.

Maddie held up one of two matching wool Fair Isle sweaters—shrunk to the point of no return. "I ruined both of these."

Zoe shrugged, looking unconcerned.

"Were they a gift?" Maddie knew sweaters like this were not cheap. The brand-name label proved it.

Jackson was not going to be happy.

Zoe cocked her head. "I think Grandma got them for us, but they were really itchy."

Maddie held up the other one, obviously Dora's. It was even smaller. "They are doll sized now."

Zoe grabbed one and stuck it on her head, giggling. "Maybe I can wear it as a hat."

Maddie smiled, but her insides cringed. Gifts from their grandmother, ruined. Jackson was going to be mad.

She glanced at the clock showing almost four thirty. He'd be home in a little more than an hour. Should she make dinner as an olive branch?

She glanced at Dora, who had taken her tiny sweater and placed it on her head too.

"Look, Sissy. Same hats."

Zoe laughed.

An idea flashed through Maddie's brain so fast that she rubbed her forehead. Then she held out her hand. "Let me see one of those. Please."

"Take mine." Zoe offered hers.

Dora still wore hers on her head while she crunched the last bit of apple.

Maddie looked over the now-felted wool, turning it inside then back out. She stuck her hand inside. It would make a supercute pair of mittens.

She slipped Dora's shrunken sweater off her head and chuckled at the static left behind on the four-year-old's brown curls that stuck out every which way. "I think I can make something out of these. But first, I'll have to show your dad."

"How come?" Zoe asked.

"Because I need to ask if I can cut them up."

Zoe grinned. "Can I help?"

"Me too?" Dora asked.

"We'll see what your dad says." Maddie set the two sweaters aside, then finished folding the rest of the clothes, stacking them neatly in the basket.

Once that was done, she padded to the fridge and scanned its contents. A package of four chicken breasts looked like they had been thawed for dinner. She could do chicken. In fact, she made a creamy Tuscan-style chicken dish that was quick, easy and pretty fabulous. That ought to smooth the wrinkles of her carelessly shrunken sweaters. It used to work on Stan; she hoped it worked on Jackson too.

Scanning the condiments on the door, she spotted a jar of sun-dried tomatoes and a block of Parmesan cheese. Perfect. In the produce drawers, she found a bag of spinach and some garlic bulbs. On the top shelf, next to the milk, stood a carton of half-and-half. She'd rather have heavy cream, but she'd make do.

Maddie gathered up all her ingredients and set them on the counter, then turned to the girls. "Do you like chicken in a creamy sauce with pasta?"

Zoe's eyes widened. "Are you going to make dinner?"

"I sure am."

"I like chicken," Dora said.

"Me too." Zoe stepped close to the counter. "Can I help?"

"You may. First thing I'll need is a big frying pan. Do you know where they are?"

Zoe nodded and went to a bottom cupboard and opened it. "They're in here."

"Perfect." Maddie pulled the largest one out and got to work sautéing the chicken. Then she found a two-pound box of fettuccine pasta from the walk-in pantry.

Zoe helped with measurements, while Dora handed her ingredients from her perch on a pulled-up chair to the counter next to the stove. It wasn't long before she heard Jackson enter the house.

"Something smells amazing." He tossed his keys on the counter and crept up behind her, peering over her shoulder since each girl stood on either side of her. "Maddie, what are you making?"

"Creamy Tuscan chicken." His nearness made her jittery, and she dropped the wooden spoon on the floor with a splat. She didn't dare bend down to retrieve it or she'd bump right into him.

"We're helping." Dora reached her hands out for her father to pick her up.

He did so and moved away. "Wow, you girls are good helpers."

Fortunately, Zoe picked up the spoon.

"They are. Thank you, Zoe. You can put that in the sink and I'll get another one." Maddie tried to gather her wits. Nervous about the sweaters and thrown off-kilter by the warm feel of Jackson standing so close had her in a tizzy.

She turned down the heat and covered the pan of chicken swimming in creamy sauce with spinach and tomatoes. She checked the pot of water for the pasta, but it wasn't yet boiling. "Zoe, do you want to set the table with silverware? I'll get the plates and glasses."

"Sure." Zoe pulled open the drawer with a rattle and fished out forks and butter knives.

"Anything I can do?" Jackson stood apart from them, still holding Dora.

"No." Maddie couldn't look at him.

Those sweaters sitting on top of the basket of folded clothes taunted her, whispering how angry Jackson was going to be when she showed him. Tamping down nerves, she kept busy setting out three plates and three glasses.

"That's not right," he said.

Maddie looked up quick. "What?"

"It's four settings, not three. You're going to eat with us, aren't you? I mean, you made it." His smile was warm and not the least bit threatening. In fact, he looked so relaxed and happy, she hated to disrupt his night with her laundry error.

Maddie bit her lip. It might be easier to broach the

shrunken sweaters after a good meal. "Okay, four settings."

She grabbed another plate and hoped for the best.

Jackson sat back, feeling stuffed. He actually sighed with contentment, something he hadn't done in a long while. "That was great."

This past week, coming home from work had become a pleasure he looked forward to. Maddie had filled his house with joy and calm, steady warmth. He didn't have to worry about what mood might greet him at the door. Or what emotional disaster. She'd even done the girls' laundry, and her chicken dinner was far superior to anything he might have made. The girls had liked it. They liked everything about Maddie.

He did too.

"I'm glad you enjoyed it." Maddie rose and started gathering up the dishes.

"Can we watch TV?" Zoe asked.

"Sure, honey, go ahead." Jackson wouldn't mind talking with Maddie privately.

He should tell her to let him do cleanup duty, but then she'd leave. He didn't want her to go. He liked watching her move around his kitchen. He'd missed having a woman other than his mother or sister cook a really good meal. He did okay on his own, but not as good as what Maddie had whipped up.

The girls ran to the living room, and he heard the sound of the TV in the distance. Zoe changed the channel from the local news to old cartoons.

He stood and helped clear the table, bringing glasses toward the sink, where Maddie took charge of loading the dishwasher. "Here you go."

"Thanks." Maddie kept her head down and focused a little too intently on her task. She seemed tense.

"Is everything okay?"

"I have something to show you." Her voice sounded tight, and she actually rolled her shoulders before rinsing her hands.

He watched as she dried her hands and then marched toward the basket of neatly folded clothes he'd spotted near the door when he'd arrived. "Thanks for doing laundry, by the way. You don't have to do that."

"Don't thank me just yet. I accidentally shrunk these." She held up the girls' matching sweaters. The ones his mom had bought them for Christmas last year.

Jackson looked at her closely.

She chewed her bottom lip and barely met his gaze. Had she been nervous to tell him?

"Maddie, it's no big deal. I don't think the girls liked wearing them anyway."

"But they were a gift, weren't they?" Maddie set them back down and walked toward him, finally looking him in the eyes.

"From their grandmother." He wasn't going to fib about it.

"I'm so sorry." Contrition showed from the depths of her blue eyes, along with worry. Had she been afraid of his reaction?

Now he was sorry for telling her the truth. "Don't worry about it, really."

She pushed her glasses back up the bridge of her nose. "Well, I have an idea to remake them into a hat-and-mitten set for Zoe. Do you mind if I take them with me?"

"Sure, go for it. I can finish up here, if you need to head home." Jackson still didn't want her to leave, but he really should let her go.

"Okay." She looked relieved. Whether that relief came from leaving or his lack of anger at the shrunken sweaters, he wasn't sure.

The yearbook photos he'd seen flashed through his mind, and he had to know about the jock he'd seen. "Maddie, where did you meet your late husband?"

She looked surprised and then guarded. "Here, in high school. Why?"

He shrugged. "Just curious."

"Where did you meet your wife?" Her eyes challenged him, making her look more like her senior picture.

*Touché.*

"At my first teaching job downstate. Delia was a music teacher too. She taught elementary while I taught in the middle school."

Instead of leaving, Maddie entered the kitchen and resumed her stance at the sink. She rinsed their dinner plates and loaded them into the dishwasher. "Were the sweaters from Delia's mother?"

*Is she still worried about that?*

"No. Delia's parents moved back to Greece. I don't have much contact with them. The sweaters were from my mom."

"So that explains the girls' names. They're Greek." Maddie smiled.

"As soon as we found out Delia was pregnant, she had Zoe's name picked out. Not sure what would have happened if we'd had a boy." Jackson had the table cleared and reached for the dishcloth. His elbow brushed Maddie's arm as he rinsed it in hot water. The awareness of her standing so close gave him pause, but he took his time rinsing off that dishcloth.

"Jackson Junior?"

He chuckled as he wrung the cloth out and finally stepped away from her. "Nope, not doing that."

"It's a nice name," she said softly.

"After my grandfather. What about your full name of Madelyn?"

"My grandmother's." Maddie had finished with the dishes. She reached under the sink for a soap pod, popped it in and started the dishwasher.

He wiped down the table, then wadded up the cloth and tossed it in the sink basketball-style. He knew better than to stand so close again.

Maddie grabbed it, rinsed it, then hung it over the edge of the sink. Nothing was left out of place with her around.

"How long were you and Stan married?" It just came out.

Her eyes widened. "How'd you know his name was Stan?"

*Busted.*

"The band room has a bunch of yearbooks. I was riffling through one when I saw your senior picture."

A shadow seemed to cross over her face, darkening her expression and dulling her eyes. "We eloped right out of high school, after Stan had enlisted."

"Wow." Seven years, and yet no kids. Jackson knew better than to ask why. It was far too personal a question, and Jackson had already pushed that line enough.

"Yes, wow. Neither of our parents wanted us to get married, but..." She shrugged. "I better head home."

He followed Maddie as she walked toward the side porch, scooping up the two sweaters on her way. He grabbed her jacket hanging on the hall tree while she folded those sweaters into her purse. He held the down coat open for her. "Look, I'm sorry if I crossed a line."

She stared at his hands holding her coat as if debating

whether she should slip into it or not. Finally, she did. When she turned to face him, Maddie looked calm and collected, as if she'd closed the blinds on that part of her life. "It's okay."

He knew it wasn't. "I didn't purposefully look you up, Maddie. I was checking out the band pictures and flipped to the next page and there you were."

She smiled, but it was a sad smile filled with regret and secrets. "That was a long time ago and I'm not that girl anymore."

That much was obvious, but Jackson wasn't sure if Maddie meant it as a good thing or not. He worried that it wasn't good. She'd said that they'd eloped after their families had disapproved. That showed some gumption and outright rebellion. He didn't know what he'd do if one of his daughters pulled a stunt like that.

"Night."

His thoughts scattered as she exited to the side porch and jogged across their two driveways. Was she running from him or her memories?

"Good night, Maddie. Sleep tight," he whispered long after she'd gone into her house.

They'd lifted the lid on their past lives and loves, but neither one had peered in too deep. That was probably a good thing, because his past was still a source of sleepless nights. He wouldn't be surprised if Maddie's situation was similar.

Sunday morning, Maddie made her way up front after service as if a string had pulled her there. The pastor had opened up the altar for anyone and everyone to pray, lay down their spiritual burdens or simply bask in God's presence a little longer.

As she dodged the pumpkins that decorated the steps,

Maddie did a little of all three. Once again, she asked forgiveness for hating Stan. And once again, she felt unworthy to accept it. This morning she'd shifted her prayers to Jackson and the girls, wanting to protect them from any more harm and heal the wounds she knew must remain.

Friday, before leaving the Taylor house, Maddie had offered to take Zoe and Dora to the Harvest Party held at her church. She'd even invited Jackson along when he didn't answer right away, but he'd refused.

He'd had a perfectly good excuse, though. He was taking the girls back to Escanaba for the weekend and they were staying with his parents. She'd even made a joke about not telling his mom what she'd done to the girls' sweaters to lighten the conversation, but Jackson had looked hard around the edges when she'd mentioned the word *church*.

Maddie felt a hand on her shoulder and looked up.

Erica smiled. "You okay? I can pray with you."

"Oh, I'm fine. Finished, actually, but thank you." She rose to her feet.

Erica did too. "Then come. Ruth is still here and there's coffee left in the foyer."

"I could use another cup." Maddie laughed. She'd been running late this morning and had managed to down only one mug while she worked on those hat-and-mitten sets.

Saturday, she'd scoured the local thrift stores for wool sweaters and had found several. It didn't feel right giving only Zoe a hat-and-mitten set, so Maddie planned out a set for Dora as well.

Interchanging wool from the girls' sweaters with other woolens she'd washed and dried, she'd easily come out with two matching sets. She wanted to finish them up today, so she could present them to the girls tonight. They could wear them to school the following day, as Novem-

ber first promised to be cold but dry. No snow had been
forecast for the upcoming week. Maddie could remember blizzards in mid-October when she was a kid. To be
so cold yet no snow was unusual.

"Hey, Maddie." Ruth gave her a hug. "How's the nanny
job?"

"Good." Maddie grinned. "I guess I *am* a nanny."

"I imagine a very good one too." Erica handed them
each a pressed paper cup of coffee still hot from this
morning.

"The girls make it easy. They are such sweeties." Maddie loved those two girls. She knew she would, but she
hadn't figured on the sense of purpose they gave her.

"And their dad?" Erica sipped her coffee.

"Yeah, what's he like?" Ruth added.

Maddie wasn't sure how to explain Jackson. He was
warm and caring and handsome. He'd looked her up in
the school yearbook and then found Stan. Why would he
do that if he wasn't curious about her? Interested even.
If he didn't want—

Maddie cut off that train of thought. "He's fine."

She noticed that Ruth and Erica had exchanged looks.

"No, really. He's a nice guy."

"Does he attend church around here, do you know?"
Ruth asked.

"I don't think so." Maddie didn't believe he attended
at all, and that bothered her.

She'd grown up without going to any type of church,
and she didn't want that to happen to Zoe and Dora.
Church would be good for those girls. They loved taking turns praying with her over meals. At least Jackson
hadn't put his foot down against that. He'd allowed it,
even though he didn't participate.

"Invite him," Erica said.

"Yeah, maybe." Maddie didn't think that would go over well, considering the sour look he'd given her when she'd mentioned the church Harvest Party.

"There's Nora and the boys." Ruth had spotted her mother-in-law. "I gotta run. See you at next lunch."

"'Bye." Maddie waved.

Erica waved too, before focusing back in on Maddie. "If you need anything, let me know, okay? Just call me."

"I will. Thanks." Maddie wouldn't burden her that way, but it was nice to know she had more than just her mom to lean on if needed.

She watched Erica head out, but Maddie didn't leave. She felt drawn back to the altar. Checking her watch, she had a little more time before her mother expected her for dinner. She peeked into the sanctuary. The place had thinned out, but there were a few people still lingering.

"Looking for me?" The pastor seemed to appear out of nowhere.

"Umm. No, but can I ask you a question?"

"Of course."

"How do you know if you're forgiven?" Maddie fiddled with her gloves while she waited for the answer.

The pastor considered the question carefully. "It takes faith to accept it. And sometimes it takes confession. It just depends. Is there anything you want to talk about? We can schedule an appointment this week."

Maddie shook her head. "No. That's okay. I think I'm good."

The pastor touched her arm. "Maddie, you've been through a terrible loss. We're here if you need us. The grief support group, the elders, my wife, me."

She hadn't attended the grief support group in weeks. She couldn't relate to all that sorrow when all she felt was relief, anger and bitterness. She'd wasted seven years of her life married to Stan.

"I know. Thank you." She smiled and then headed for the door to make her escape. "'Bye. Have a good week."

Once outside, she breathed in the cold air that for once refreshed rather than froze.

*Confession?*

No, no, she couldn't repeat the terrible things she'd said to Stan. Those hate-filled words hung on to her like an anchor, pulling her down. If only she could cut them loose and know they were gone forever. If only she could know she was truly forgiven for saying them without having to tell anyone what she'd said.

## Chapter Seven

Jackson returned home early Sunday evening. He'd already unpacked the car and everyone's suitcases, throwing most of their clothes into the washer. The whites were tossed in a hamper until there was a full load. Delia had taught him to separate colors from whites. She'd been a stickler on that.

Zoe and Dora were in the living room watching TV, so he ambled in to build a fire. Even though he'd turned up the thermostat when they got home, the house still felt chilly. His heart too. Sunday nights were when he missed his wife the most. Maybe because they'd always enjoyed a quiet evening as a family before the hectic week started.

Jackson grabbed a handful of kindling sticks and settled them in the grate. He struck a match and held it under the pile until flames licked the thin wood. Finally, the fire spread and he tried to kick off his melancholy. "Did you girls enjoy visiting Grandma and Grandpa?"

Dora was wrapped in a knitted throw and she sucked her two fingers. She nodded but that was all.

Zoe stared at the TV and the *Cinderella* movie playing on the screen, but she'd heard him. "It was okay."

"Just okay? How come?" Jackson chuckled as he threw a couple of small logs on top of the burning kindling.

Zoe shrugged. "Too much work."

Jackson laughed. That sounded about right. His parents were great, but their idea of entertaining the girls was having them help around the house. Raking leaves had been a big part of Saturday afternoon. At least the girls got to jump in those piles. This morning, his parents took the girls to church, but he'd stayed behind. Maybe his girls would have had more fun going with Maddie to her church's Harvest Party—

A knock at the side door interrupted his thoughts. Peeking through the long, sheer curtains, he spotted Maddie standing on the porch with a brown paper bag in her hands. Seeing her made him smile.

He went to the door and opened it. "Hi."

She was bundled up against the cold north wind blistering the area. She held out the bag. "I have something for the girls."

Jackson backed up. "Come in. Man, I wish it would snow already. That wind is bitter."

"I know." She looked hesitant, but stepped inside and held out the bag to him again.

"Come in by the fire where it's warm. The girls would love to see you, and you can give them your gift." He didn't mention how glad he was to see her or how her presence chased that melancholy feeling away.

She slipped out of her coat and hung it up.

Jackson noticed that she wore a bulky sweatshirt, but with leggings that hugged her slim frame instead of the boxy stuff she normally wore. Her hair had been pulled back into a high ponytail.

She lifted the bag. "It's the shrunken sweaters remade."

"Cool. Come on." He gestured for her to follow him into the living room. "Maddie's here with something for you."

"Yay!" Dora slid from the couch and bounded into Maddie's waiting arms.

His heart twisted at the sight.

"Hi, Maddie. We're watching *Cinderella*," Zoe informed her.

Maddie lifted Dora to her hip and smiled. "I see that. I have something for you and your sister."

"What is it?" Zoe asked.

"Come see." Maddie held out the bag to his seven-year-old.

Zoe hit Pause on the remote and popped up to grab the bag. She pulled out a hat that had a pair of mittens stuffed inside. "It's the sweaters."

"Yup." Maddie grinned. "That one is yours, and there's a smaller set for Dora. Try them on so I can see if they fit."

Jackson watched as Zoe donned the colorful woolen hat and matching mittens. They fit great. He reached in the bag for Dora's set and looked them over. The hat and mittens were a patchwork of the shrunken Fair Isle and a solid bright blue. The squares had been melded together, but the insides were lined with matching blue fleece. A blue fur pom-pom sprouted from the top of the hat.

He flipped the mittens over. "How'd you make these?"

His youngest reached for her set. "Mine."

"I know, honey." Jackson obliged by slipping the hat on Dora's head and that brought him very close to a smiling Maddie. She looked proud, and rightly so. He slid the mittens on Dora's little hands. "These are really nice."

"Thanks. I bought some wool sweaters at a thrift store and worked them in so I could make two sets."

He stepped back and saw that a few strands of Maddie's hair were clinging to the arm of his sweater. He laughed.

She did too, but she backed up, severing the connection. *Too bad.*

"Look, Sissy." Dora held up her mitten-clad hands.

Zoe turned and showed off her mittens and hat that had been stitched with a bright red wool with matching red fleece and pom-pom on top. Red and blue were colors found in the original shrunken sweaters.

"Maddie, I'm really impressed. You could sell these. In fact, you *should* sell these. The high school is having a craft fair as a fundraiser for band next weekend. You could have a table."

"You really think people would buy these?" Maddie tipped her head. Her ponytail was still full of static and sticking out, as if reaching for him.

He was tempted to comply and move closer, but didn't dare. "Yeah, I think so. Could you make a dozen in a week?"

Maddie considered the question. "I'll need more wool sweaters for sure, but maybe. Now that I have a pattern of sorts made up, it's just a matter of cutting and sewing and embellishing."

"Wanna watch *Cinderella*?" Zoe had resumed the movie. She knelt on the floor but didn't take off her hat or mittens.

"Stay," Jackson prompted before she could refuse. "I've got pizzas ordered for delivery. More than enough."

Dora had put her head on Maddie's shoulder. The pom-pom of Dora's hat rubbed against Maddie's face, caressing her perfectly shaped lips.

"That tickles." Maddie pulled the hat off Dora and the mittens too and handed them over to Jackson. "She looks ready to nap."

Jackson took the woolens from Zoe and placed them

back in the bag with Dora's. "You can wear them tomorrow to school."

"Awwwww." Zoe hung her head back.

Maddie sat down on the couch, still holding a sleepy Dora, and covered her up with the knitted throw his sister had given them. "I guess I'm staying."

"Yay!" Zoe hopped up onto the couch next to her.

Jackson raised the bag with the gifts she'd made. "I'll put these away. Maddie, can I get you something to drink?"

"Sure. I'll take a root beer if you have it."

"You got it." Jackson took in the scene of his girls cuddled on the couch with Maddie and winced.

He wished for things that were way too soon to even contemplate, like how nicely Maddie fit into their little family of three. His girls loved her, and if he wasn't careful, he might fall in love with her too.

The next day, Maddie had Dora at her house for the afternoon while she made a few more hat-and-mitten sets. She definitely needed more sweaters if she was going to have a table at the craft fair, but she'd managed to crank out three sets today. She'd even felted one of her old wool sweaters just to get that third set done.

"Hellloooo," Pearl squawked from the perch in Maddie's sewing room.

"Hello, Pearl," Dora responded. She sat on the floor in a puddle of sunshine with a pair of child scissors, cutting up an old skirt pattern that Maddie had never used. "You're a pwetty bird."

Maddie chuckled at Dora's lisp.

"Pretty bird. Pretty." Pearl loved being talked to and Dora had warmed up to the parrot, going so far as to finally pet her.

"Nice job, Dora." Maddie added the finishing touches of buttons on the mittens and pom-poms on the hats.

"Yup."

Pearl whistled and clicked. She wanted in on the conversation.

"Did you have fun with your grandparents?" Maddie asked.

Dora nodded, but kept cutting.

"What did you do?"

She shrugged. "We jumped in weaves and went to church."

Maddie raised her eyebrows. "You did? Do you like to go to church?"

Dora nodded. "Daddy don't."

"Hmm. That's too bad." Maddie wasn't surprised.

Last night, Maddie had wanted to ask Jackson if she could take his girls with her to church on Sunday mornings, but had chickened out. He hadn't minded her saying grace over the pizza, but that was quick and harmless.

*Last night.*

Maddie sighed. She'd felt part of their family, watching *Cinderella* and eating pizza. She hadn't wanted to go home, where only Pearl kept her company. Crawling into bed had felt awfully lonely too and cold. Not that she'd ever minded before. But now—

A quick knock at her front door was followed by Jackson's deep voice. "Hello? Maddie?"

Her stomach flipped over. "We're in the sewing room."

Dora went running. "Daddy!"

He picked her up in the hallway.

Zoe dashed into the room. "Hi, Pearl."

"Hellloooo." Pearl dipped her head, inviting a pet.

Zoe didn't hesitate to gently scratch her neck.

Jackson entered carrying his youngest. "Dora says she was helping you."

"She's good at cutting patterns." Maddie nodded toward the floor and then held up a pair of mittens. "She's very good company while I make these."

"Nice." Jackson's presence seemed to make the room feel warmer and smaller but better. "I have an application for the craft fair. There's plenty of room for you to have a table. And if you fill it out now, I'll take it with me tomorrow. Just so you know, I had at least three women ask me where I bought Zoe's hat and mittens."

Maddie rose from her seat. "Let's go into the kitchen and I'll fill it out now. Pearl needs a snack anyway. Zoe, would you like to feed her?"

Zoe's beautiful dark eyes widened and she looked at her dad. "Can I?"

"Sure, honey."

"Come, Pearl." Zoe held out her hand and the parrot flew right for her.

Jackson's jaw dropped. "When did she learn how to do that?"

Maddie laughed. "They've been over here a few times."

Jackson followed Maddie and Zoe into the kitchen. And Pearl stayed on the girl's hand the whole way, until Zoe deposited her onto the back of the high chair.

"You know where to find the bag of chop, right?" Maddie asked.

"Yes, I do."

"Good job." Maddie handed Zoe a small dish.

Jackson reached into his coat pocket and offered up a piece of paper. "The application."

Maddie took it, sat down and started filling it out. When she got to the bottom of the form, she spotted an amount for an application fee and rose. "I have to get my purse and write a check."

Jackson stalled her with a touch. "Nope. I got it. I'm the one who told you to do it."

"So?" Maddie stayed still. She didn't want to break the connection of Jackson's warm hand on her shoulder.

"So, I've already written the check and gave it to the coordinator to secure your spot."

"Well, thank you. I'll donate a portion of my sales, then." Maddie wanted to contribute something more than just her time and talent.

"I also left a bag with a couple of my old sweaters by the door. Consider it my donation to your materials." He winked at her and then held out his hand for Zoe. "Come on, girls. Let's head home. Tell Maddie thank you and good-night."

"'Bye, Maddie." Dora waved.

Zoe had given Pearl her food. She gave Maddie a quick hug. "'Bye, Maddie. 'Bye, Pearl."

"'Bye, 'bye." The parrot followed up with a whistle, then went back to eating her chop.

"I'll walk you out. Dora's coat is hanging in the front closet." Maddie handed over the completed craft-fair application. "I'll be there Saturday morning at nine to set up."

"Thank you for doing this. I owe you one." Jackson helped Dora into her coat.

"You paid for my application. So, no, you don't." No sooner had Maddie said it than she regretted not leveraging the opportunity to ask about taking the girls with her to church. She supposed that request could keep for now.

Maddie handed Zoe her coat. The seven-year-old slipped into it by herself. "I'll see you tomorrow."

"Good night, Maddie." Jackson smiled, then corralled his girls and headed outside.

Maddie closed the front door behind them. Leaning down, she opened the bag and pulled out the two sweaters Jackson had given her. She would felt them by washing and then drying. One of the sweaters was an odd pattern of color blocks. No wonder he didn't wear it. But the other sweater was the one he'd worn last night. A neutral tan.

She held the wool to her nose and inhaled his scent. Faint but still clinging to the fibers, it smelled of spice and citrus. She slipped the sweater on over her head, pushing her hands through the sleeves. It was too big for her, but not terribly so. She inhaled his scent once again and wrapped her arms around herself. It might not be a real embrace, but it was still welcomed, the wool soft and warm. And stupid, because it made her imagine being held for real by Jackson Taylor, her secret Romeo.

"Get a grip, Maddie. That's not going to happen." She returned to the kitchen, pulling off Jackson's sweater as she walked.

She stuffed both sweaters into the washing machine along with her own clothes to make a full load. After hitting Start, she was cleaning up Pearl's mess when she heard the soft sounds of a piano being played. Not Zoe's lessons, but expert playing. Jackson?

Despite the cold, she opened the kitchen window over the sink, hoping to hear more clearly. Maddie didn't recognize the melody, but her heart responded. It was as if every keystroke Jackson played dug deeper into her soul and beckoned to the longing buried there.

What thoughts ran through his head when he played such a poignant song? It was the kind of music one might play when missing a loved one. Most likely his late wife.

Maddie's heart pinched with envy. What would it be

like to be loved like that? Wearing Jackson's sweater was one thing, but longing to be the object of such yearning music was asking for big trouble. The heartbreak kind of trouble.

"Zoe, you can watch TV for half an hour before your lesson." Jackson sat down at the piano while his daughters watched their favorite after-school cartoon.

He liked to have piano lessons out of the way before dinner. Sometimes it worked, but more times than not, it didn't. He ran his fingers over the keys, flipped the music book open to Chopin's "Spring Waltz" and started to play. He'd played this piece many times before, so he barely had to follow the sheet music.

Delia had loved Chopin. The "Spring Waltz" had been her favorite. She'd played it often in honor of her preferred season of spring. Delia had looked forward to the daffodils blooming. She'd planted new ones every fall and their yard in Escanaba had been covered with them.

Once again, they'd bloom without her next year.

His fingers gliding, Jackson asked God yet again, *Why?* No answers came, so he kept playing, getting lost in the music. Delia had had so much to live for and yet she threw all of that away. Why?

He wasn't going down that dark road of what he'd done wrong or could have done better. It was a dead end he'd traveled too many times. His counselor had told him that more than once.

He'd spent months torturing himself with the "what if" questions—what if he'd done this or that differently, what if he'd seen the signs, what if he'd been a better husband. The guilt wasn't completely gone, but with his counselor's help, he'd learned to find some measure of acceptance, even though he knew the pain would never completely disappear.

Which always led him back to question God yet again.

Maddie might know. She had a strong faith he appreciated. Opening up to her about Delia might be awkward, especially since Maddie wasn't exactly an open book herself. But his sister had been spot-on when it came to Maddie with his girls. She was a natural caregiver. Was it a coincidence that he'd moved next door to someone like her or something else?

A scripture verse in Isaiah whispered through his mind. *For my thoughts are not your thoughts, neither are your ways my ways, saith the Lord.*

The passage didn't help, but Jackson got the message. The more he tried to control his life, the less control he had. Still, he wasn't handing over his keys just yet, so to speak. He'd trusted God in the past and ended up a widower and his daughters without their mom.

He stopped playing. Time for lessons.

"Okay, Zoe, let's go." He waited.

He heard Zoe click off the TV and pad her way into the dining room. A second set of footsteps followed and both girls stood at his left elbow.

"Can I play too?" Dora asked.

He looked at his youngest. "You really want to learn?"

"Yup." Dora grinned.

Zoe stifled a giggle. "She can play some scales."

Jackson laughed as he lifted Dora up onto his lap, knowing it would be his hands guiding his baby's fingers. "Sure, why not?"

Zoe settled on the bench to his left and warmed up with playing scales, starting with C major, then G major and so on.

Dora reached out and tried to copy her sister but hit a sour note.

Jackson laughed. "Here, let's try this. Zoe, you play the lower half, and we'll take the upper half of the scale."

They made a game of practice, and if Zoe didn't learn anything new, at least she had fun. Jackson did too. Hearing his girls giggle made it all worth it. Sometimes, fun was more important than lessons.

He was learning that well. His girls needed fun and so did he. This weekend, they'd go to the high school craft fair, and to make it more fun, he'd invite his sister to come with them. It'd be interesting to see what kind of inventory Maddie had made.

Maybe he'd entice Maddie to join them for lunch afterward. Jackson got the feeling she could use a little more fun in her life too. If he could supply it, then all the better.

Maddie had to widen her scope of thrift stores in order to have enough wool sweaters to make more hats and mittens for the upcoming craft fair. She'd scored big in the college town of Marquette, which was only a half hour's drive away. A beautiful drive too, with blue skies, sunshine and glimpses of Lake Superior after US 41 merged with M-28. Too bad the temperature hadn't climbed out of the thirties.

About to leave for Pine, Maddie slipped into her car and pulled off the pair of mittens she'd made for herself, when an idea struck her. It would be good to touch base with the boutique owner who'd refused her clothing designs. Maybe she'd have some interest in the mitten sets. It didn't hurt to check.

She started the engine, veered right out of the Goodwill parking lot and headed for downtown Marquette. After pulling into a parking spot on the street, Maddie got out, grabbed her mittens and adjusted the matching hat she'd made. She entered the shop and inhaled the faint scent of lavender. A couple of women milled around, riffling through clothing displays.

"Can I help you?" the owner asked, then smiled with recognition. "Hello, Maddie. What brings you in today?"

Maddie pulled off her hat and mittens. "I was in the neighborhood and wondered if you'd have any interest in carrying these?"

The owner looked them over. "Did you make them?"

"I did. I have more too." Maddie pulled out her cell phone and displayed a picture of the several other sets she'd made.

"These are adorable."

One of the shoppers ambled close by and gushed, "Oh, I want a pair of these. Are they for sale?"

Maddie watched the owner's eyes light up. Customer interest was always a good sign.

"Not yet, but maybe soon." The owner held up her finger, gesturing for Maddie to wait while she took a quick phone call.

Maddie spoke to the shopper. "I'm selling them at the Pine High School craft fair this Saturday, if you're interested. All the info is on the Pine Public Schools' website."

"Cool." The woman returned to her shopping.

The owner completed her call and focused back on Maddie. "It's interesting that you should stop by. I'm looking to expand into the space next door. It's a very small expansion, but the person who was going to invest in that just bailed on me. Would you have any interest in buying into this place? It'd only be a thirty percent share, but it's a way to establish these." She lifted Maddie's mittens. "I think woolens like these would be a perfect fit here."

Maddie's heart started pumping hard. This was what she'd wanted for so long. Even if it meant making accessories instead of clothing, it would be a start that could lead to more. "What about my clothes?"

The owner shrugged. "Maybe, down the road. Right now, I am inundated with clothing. The woolens, I think, will hit big. Especially with the college crowd."

Maddie was definitely interested. "I'd like to see the details."

"Of course. I still have your email, so I can send you the proposal to look over. Call me with any questions and let me know for sure in a month's time, okay?"

"Thank you. I'll be in touch." Maddie reached out her hand for a firm shake.

She made it out of the store without whooping or breaking into a happy dance, but once in her car, Maddie let loose a loud *wahoo*. And then the questions she didn't think to ask swirled through her thoughts. Could she bring Pearl to the store? Maddie had a travel cage. And what hours would she work, or could she hire someone to sell for her? Shaking her head, she forced herself to calm down. Once she read the proposal, she'd seek answers for the rest.

Maddie started her car and headed for Pine. First, she'd pick up Dora. One more question popped into Maddie's thoughts—what if Dora didn't get into the daycare attached to her preschool? She couldn't leave Jackson hanging. One more thing Maddie would need to figure out before buying into that boutique.

Dora would attend kindergarten all day next year, so there was that. Her job as nanny would last only a few months after the New Year at most. But she was getting way ahead of herself. Jackson might have other plans for

Dora's care after the holidays if the daycare didn't have room. Maddie was only a temporary fix. She needed to remember that.

## Chapter Eight

The morning of the craft fair, Jackson made pancakes for the girls while they waited for their aunt to arrive. He'd told his sister about Maddie having a table for her handmade hat-and-mitten sets, and Mel had been excited to come and check it out.

"When's Aunt Mel going to be here?" Zoe twirled a bit of pancake in a pool of syrup on her plate.

Jackson glanced at the big farmhouse clock Melanie had given him when he'd visited his parents last weekend. He appreciated her explanation that she'd seen it and just had to buy it for him. It did look nice on the wall.

"Soon, honey. She left her house over half an hour ago." Jackson looked out the window over the sink and spotted Maddie carrying a large basket to her car.

He hurried to the side door, opened it and yelled out. "Do you need help?"

She looked up. Her glasses had slid halfway down her nose, so she pushed them back in place. "No. I got it. I'm heading for the high school to set up."

"We'll be there a little later."

"Great! See you there." She smiled, lighting up her whole face. The cold sunshine turned her blond hair into spun gold where it peeked out from beneath one of the patchwork hats she'd made.

Jackson wanted to know if that hair was as soft as it looked.

*Don't go there.*

He couldn't afford to. The girls were happy in Maddie's care, and he didn't want to mess that up with any unwelcome romantic overtures. He needed to keep their relationship friendly and that was it. Friends didn't run their fingers through each other's hair.

He clenched his hands into fists as he watched Maddie start her car and back out of the driveway. He needed to get a handle on those impulses before he did something they'd both regret. Besides, there were more pancakes to make and he could use a second cup of coffee.

At the stove, he poured batter onto the hot griddle and tried to shape the gloppy mess into Mickey Mouse. Delia used to make them for the girls and she'd been a pro. He still couldn't make pancakes as fluffy as hers. His wife had been a good cook, when she cooked.

He sighed, missing her. No, he missed the good times they'd had. The bad were better left forgotten. He had to own that the last couple of years there'd been more bad times than good. What memories would Zoe and Dora keep of their mom? They didn't talk about her as much as they used to.

These last couple of months, the girls had grown louder and more lively—just like little girls should be. And since Maddie had come into their lives, both Zoe and Dora giggled more. Moving to Pine had been the right decision.

He heard a car pull into the driveway, flipped the pancakes and then peeked out the window over the sink. His sister had arrived. "Aunt Mel is here."

"Aunt Mel!" Zoe raced to the side door.

Dora followed, her footed jammies making a swishing sound on the vinyl plank floors as she ran.

He heard his sister's voice greeting the girls as she entered the house. He could hear her kick off her shoes, and no doubt, she was hanging up her coat too.

"Want some breakfast?" he called out.

Melanie entered the kitchen. "Sure. It smells good."

"Pancakes and sausage." Jackson deposited a pancake onto a plate along with a couple of sausage links and handed it to her. "Butter and syrup are on the table. Coffee fixings too."

He glanced at his girls' plates. Zoe's had a couple of bites of pancake left. Dora's still had sausage. "Are you done? Zoe? Dora?"

"Nope." Dora climbed back into her booster seat and grabbed a now-cold link with her fingers and bit into it.

Melanie laughed. "Oh, to be a child who didn't care about the temperature of food."

Jackson poured more batter onto the grill for himself. The sausages were staying warm in the oven. He turned it off. "Zoe?"

"Yeah, I'm done." His eldest daughter turned to her aunt. "We're going to a craft fair."

"I know. That's why I'm here. Hoping to pick up some Christmas presents." His sister poured syrup over her pancake.

"For me?" Zoe asked.

Melanie tapped the end of Zoe's nose. "Maybe."

His daughter smiled.

Jackson did too, even though he didn't relish the upcoming holidays—the second set without his wife. He and the girls were heading for his parents' house for both Thanksgiving and Christmas, just like last year. Maybe, just maybe, this year would be less sore and a little happier. He hoped so.

Thoughts of where Maddie might spend the holidays wound through his mind. Did she have family in the area to celebrate those days with? He wasn't sure. If not, he'd figure something out, because there was no way he'd let her face her first holidays as a widow all alone.


Maddie dropped two hat-and-mitten sets into a plain brown gift bag and handed it to a middle-aged woman who'd raved about them. "Here you go. And thank you for your purchase."

"My pleasure. These will make perfect gifts." The woman smiled as she clutched the bag and left.

Maddie looked over her dwindling product supply. In the two hours since she'd set up, she'd sold more than expected. She'd even bumped the price a little, considering it was for a good cause, and yet they still flew off her table. That proved she could probably charge even more. All things to consider for buying into that boutique in Marquette.

She'd read through the emailed proposal, spent an hour on the phone with the owner going over questions and then promised to get back to her once she figured out the finances. Maddie didn't have enough in her savings to make it happen, so she'd have to see about a loan. A loan she'd need approval for by the end of the month.

"Maddie, these are amazing!" Erica Laine stood before her table and scooped up two more sets. "For my daughters for Christmas. They'll love them."

"Thanks." She smiled and made change, but Erica refused the cash back.

"Consider that my donation to the band," Erica said.

"Okay, done." Maddie slipped the bills into a separate pocket of her fanny pack. Several people had done the same thing. The Pine community had always been a generous one.

"Hi, Maddie." Zoe ran up to her table.

"Zoe!" Maddie looked around, and sure enough, Jackson, Melanie and Dora were not far behind.

Dora wiggled out of Jackson's hold on her hand and darted straight for her, arms wide.

Maddie scooped her up into a hug. "Hi, sweetie."

Erica smiled. "Are these the girls you watch after school? They're adorable."

"They are. Zoe, Dora, this is Erica Laine." Maddie saw that Jackson and Melanie were within hearing distance and extended the introduction. "Erica, this is Jackson Taylor and his sister, Melanie."

Erica shook each of their hands. "Nice to meet you both."

"Are you Maddie's mom?" Zoe asked.

Maddie felt her face heat, even though Erica was three years older than her forty-five-year-old mother. "No."

"No." Erica laughed at their unison answer. "I'm her friend. We go to the same church."

"Yes." Flustered, Maddie merely nodded in agreement.

"Can we go to your church?" Zoe asked.

Dora stood with her fingers in her mouth, but she nodded in agreement. That little one followed her sister's lead a lot.

Maddie's gaze flew to Jackson.

He shifted, looking uncomfortable. "We'll see."

Erica didn't waste a moment to zero in on that discomfort. "Maddie tells me you recently moved here. Have you found a congregation yet?"

"Uh, no. Not yet." Jackson smiled politely, but he was

clearly not interested, which was too bad. His girls needed to be in church. He did too.

"Well, Maddie can vouch for the place, if you'd like to give us a try." Erica glanced at her watch. "I better run. I'm working a later shift today. It was really nice meeting you."

"The same," Jackson said.

His sister agreed.

"Can we go to your church tomorrow?" Zoe bounced up and down.

Maddie glanced at Jackson's sister before focusing back on him. "They have a great kids program."

"We'll see." Jackson wouldn't commit, but he didn't look angry. His gaze remained friendly but closed. "You've done well today?"

At the change of subject, Maddie knew when to back off. She'd had a lot of experience not pushing too hard with Stan. "Yes, I've nearly sold out."

Melanie grabbed her last three sets. "Now you're sold out."

"You don't have to do that," Maddie blustered.

"Gifts for friends. They'll love them. And a set for me."

Maddie smiled. "Thank you. The third set is on the house."

Melanie still paid for it. "Give my share to the band, then."

She laughed. "Okay, okay. I will."

Jackson gently tapped on her table. "We're going to look around for a bit and then head for ice cream at that sweetshop in town, maybe lunch after. Would you like to join us?"

Maddie never turned down ice cream. The fact that they were going for sweets before lunch made her laugh.

Jackson did that a lot. "Yes. That'd be fun. I have to pack up here. I could meet you there."

"I'll text you when we're on our way." Jackson hesitated a moment while his sister and the girls wandered over to another table filled with doll clothes. "Thank you again for doing this."

"I loved every minute." Maddie wasn't fibbing. Selling something she'd made was great, but hearing the positive comments on her work was downright exhilarating. She was definitely onto something with these woolen accessories.

"I can see that."

She tipped her head.

"You're practically glowing," Jackson added, his voice soft. "And it looks good on you."

The compliment warmed her all the way down to her toes. "Thank you."

"See you in a bit."

"Yes." Maddie got lost in the blue depths of his eyes as she sought any deception in his compliment. She didn't find any.

He broke eye contact and tapped her table again before walking away to catch up with his sister and his girls.

Maddie watched him go, her heart beating fast in her chest. A little flame had been ignited between them, just a tiny flicker of heat that might grow if they fanned the spark.

But should they? Sparks had a way of turning into a bonfire if not controlled, and Maddie wasn't exactly wise when it came to men.

Sunday morning, Jackson found himself in Maddie's church sitting next to her. Well, not quite. Dora was scrunched between them. As much as he didn't want to attend, he'd conceded that his girls very much wanted to and he couldn't slough that duty off on Maddie. A good father brought his children to church. He figured that it'd be beneficial for the girls to make friends here, but deep down, he knew it was much more than that. Even Zoe knew church was more than seeing friends.

Hearing his seven-year-old sing her little heart out during the song service had nearly broken him. She knew many of the songs and he'd kept her away too long because of his issues. His anger. It was time to right that wrong.

They switched gears to sing an old hymn, and he caught the sound of Maddie's voice mixing in with the rest. She had a bright voice that was right on pitch. She didn't harmonize, but carried the melody well.

The music wasn't bad, but part of him wanted to volunteer to make it better. That would have to keep for now. He was dipping his toes back into church attendance. There was no way he'd jump in without first testing the water. Only fools rushed in, even when it came to church.

The minister stepped up to make announcements and to dismiss the kids for children's church.

"Should I go?" Zoe quietly asked.

"Do you want to?" he asked back.

She nodded.

"Okay, take your sister too, then."

"Come on, Dora." Zoe pulled on Dora's arm to no avail. Dora was firmly attached to Maddie's right arm. "Dora!"

"Nope."

Jackson chuckled in spite of the small scene they were making. "Zoe, you go ahead. Dora can go next time."

Zoe folded her arms across her chest. "She's not going to want to stay here, Daddy."

Maddie leaned down and whispered, "Would you like me to take you? I can hang around until you get used to it."

Dora glanced at him.

He nodded.

Lo and behold, Dora took Maddie's hand and Zoe latched on to her other hand. He watched the three of them walk toward the side door where the other kids had stampeded through.

He was all alone now, listening with half an ear to the minister's announcements from the altar that could also serve as a stage. Jackson let his gaze wander around the sanctuary. It was a pretty whitewashed church, with real, cushioned pews covered in navy cloth. The windows appeared to have been replaced with practical ones that could be opened. Little pumpkin cornucopias rested on the bottom ledges. Above the replacement windows were the original stained glass window toppers that were triangular in shape. No scenes, just splashes of color.

The minister began his message and Jackson homed in. It was as if the man spoke directly to him—stating that those who'd experienced exceptional loss shouldn't blame God but seek Him fervently because our days on earth were mere blips in time and eternity awaited.

Jackson tried to tune the minister out, but couldn't. The guy had a way of delivering a sermon that made a person sit up and listen. There were points Jackson would love to debate, but why bother? How was he supposed to trust in a God who let him and his girls down? A God who wouldn't speak to his despairing wife's soul when she needed help?

He felt Maddie slip back in next to him. His thoughts scattered when he caught a whiff of her light floral scent. She looked exceptionally pretty this morning in a not-quite-pink corduroy dress shaped like a pair of overalls but with a skirt. She wore a cream-colored turtleneck sweater underneath that hugged her slender shape. Her hair was twisted up into a messy knot that begged to be undone—

He slammed the brakes on those thoughts and tried to refocus on the sermon. The minister was saying something about a shepherd chasing after a lost sheep, rejoicing when it came back into the fold. Jackson wasn't a lost sheep who'd wandered; he'd purposefully stepped away with good reason. At least, he thought he had good reason. He knew he was wrong, but couldn't make things right. Who was he to tell God how things should be?

*For my thoughts are not your thoughts, neither are your ways my ways, saith the Lord.*

He gripped the edge of the pew. He wasn't ready to surrender just yet. There were too many questions and prayers left unanswered. Too much distrust.

Another song wrapped up the service and then folks began to slowly disperse. Maddie turned to him. "I can show you where to pick up the girls."

He chuckled when he spotted Zoe and Dora dodging people as they ran toward them. "No need. Here they come."

"Look what we made!" Zoe held up a piece of blue construction paper with a brown paper cutout of her hand glued on top to look like a turkey. The fingers were colored and decorated like feathers and the thumb had a red wattle for the head.

Dora held up hers. It wasn't as neat and tidy as Zoe's.

"Very nice. We can hang them up when we get home." Jackson's fridge was getting crowded with their *artwork*, but he'd make room for more.

"Nice job, girls!" Maddie added. "Those are some supercool Thanksgiving turkeys."

Jackson took the opportunity to ask, "Where are you spending Thanksgiving?"

"My mom's."

"Is she in town?"

"A few miles outside of town."

Jackson looked at Maddie. "You don't talk a lot about your mom."

"We're not as close as we should be."

"Why not?" Now he was prying. They walked toward the exit at the back of the sanctuary.

Maddie shrugged. "I never went to church growing up. I became a believer in Christ after attending a service on base. Instead of my faith drawing my mom and me closer, it pushed us further apart. She didn't want to hear about my new *religion*, as she called it."

His family had always been believers and he'd been raised going to church. "That must have been tough."

"Sometimes. Mom remarried over a year ago, while I was in North Carolina," Maddie finally said.

"And," he coaxed.

"And he's her world now."

"Don't you like your mother's husband?"

Her eyes darkened. "I don't really know him, but what I've seen so far, I'm not impressed."

"I'm sorry," Jackson offered.

"My mom doesn't have a good track record when it comes to men and marriage. My father left when I was Zoe's age and there were a few others in between. She married this one, so we'll see what happens."

Jackson had never heard bitterness in Maddie's voice before. He didn't like it. It saddened him. "We're heading to my parents' for Thanksgiving. If you'd like to join us, I'm sure Melanie would love to have you stay with her."

Maddie looked up fast, eyes now wide. "Thank you, but I need to go to my mom's. There's been too many holidays I've missed with her."

"I understand." He was glad she wasn't giving up on her relationship with her mother.

They exited the sanctuary into an open foyer where they retrieved their winter coats. Jackson bent down to zip up Dora's jacket and get her into her hat and mittens when the minister approached them.

He held out his hand. "I don't think we've met. I'm Bill Parsons, the pastor here."

Jackson straightened and returned the handshake. "Jackson Taylor. My daughters and I recently moved here. I teach music at the middle school."

Bill's eyes lit up. "If you're willing, we always need help with the music for our worship service."

Jackson wasn't opposed to helping out, but that would mean regular attendance. Glancing down at his girls, who told Maddie about all the fun they'd had in children's church, he knew resistance was futile. They needed to attend church, and it might as well be this one. "I'll keep that in mind."

"Great, and welcome. Maddie, how are you?" Bill seemed genuinely interested in her answer.

Jackson knew that tone well. His family counselor asked it the very same way. He wondered if Maddie had sought counseling with her minister. And Jackson found himself wondering if the guy was even qualified to counsel on more than spiritual issues.

"Doing well, thank you." Maddie had been warm and friendly, but Jackson knew a brush-off when he heard it. He really didn't know much about Maddie. Other than the brief comments she'd just made about her tenuous relationship with her mom, she rarely talked about herself. She never mentioned her late husband, either. Why was that? Had Stan been a brute? He'd looked the part. Jackson hoped not, but he had a bad feeling that Maddie knew her way around disappointments and heartache. He didn't like that, either.

They walked out into frigid air despite clear blue skies and sunshine. Jackson reached for Zoe's and Dora's mitten-covered hands and glanced at Maddie, walking next to them. She had her down coat collar turned up against the wind. They'd ridden together to church, so they all climbed into his car.

Jackson started the engine and let it warm up a bit before turning up the heat. "I'd rather it snow than be this cold."

Maddie laughed. "I can't say I've been warm since I moved back."

"Your blood hasn't thickened up yet." He knew it didn't get this cold in North Carolina. No wonder Maddie wore sweaters all the time. Although, seeing her without the oversized ones she usually wore was rather nice. Too nice.

"No, it sure hasn't." She turned to him then. "How did you like church?"

"I've been a churchgoer most of my life, Maddie. This wasn't anything new for me, but I will say, I like the way your minister delivers a sermon."

"He's good."

"You know him well, then?"

Maddie shrugged. "He runs a grief support group on Monday nights. I went regularly when I first started going to church here—that's where I met Erica, the woman you

met at the craft fair. She and I and another recently widowed woman meet for lunch weekly."

"Did it help?" She didn't seem racked with grief, but
then, maybe she buried it down deep or didn't like talking about it.

"A little. Meeting with Erica and Ruth helps more,
though."

"How come?"

Her smile was shy. "For one, it's easier to share with
two nice ladies versus a room full of people."

"How many meet?" Maybe he'd check it out. Or maybe
not. He didn't want to rehash everything he'd been through
when he was finally on the other side of grief.

"About six or eight."

He chuckled. Not exactly what he'd consider a roomful.
He imagined that, from Maddie's perspective, two women
who'd also lost their husbands could become close and
supportive friends. He liked knowing that she had a support system, especially since she wasn't close to her mom.

Curious, he asked, "Is your pastor licensed in family
counseling, do you know?"

Maddie shrugged. "I don't know. He must have something, since he leads the support group and folks from
outside the congregation attend."

"Hmm." Jackson figured he'd find out sooner or later.
As far as churches went, he liked this one. The girls
seemed to as well, but then, that could be because of
Maddie.

On the short drive home, he was tempted to ask her to
have dinner with them, but thought better of it. They'd
spent a lot of time together this weekend, and although
Maddie had talked more to Melanie than him, he should
probably back off a little.

Melanie and Maddie seemed to get along far better

than his late wife had with his sister. That was a good sign, wasn't it?

He needed to stop picturing Maddie as part of his family. At least for now.

They'd see her tomorrow, and they'd have dinner together on Tuesday. Maddie prepared meals on his band rehearsal days since he came home late. He smiled just thinking about it. Tuesdays and Thursdays had become his favorite days of the week.

## Chapter Nine

Maddie hummed while she fixed dinner. A song she'd heard on the radio during her drive to Dora's preschool was still stuck in her head. Lots of dah-dah-dahs and a hearts-get-broken chorus tangled through her mind. Along with too many thoughts of Jackson.

Some of those lyrics were a dead ringer for her growing fear of getting her heart broken. She loved the girls, and falling for their father didn't seem too far a stretch—if she wasn't so afraid of making another mistake.

She focused on finishing up a salad and pushed aside the nagging attraction she had for her neighbor and secret Romeo. Every Tuesday and Thursday evening, she made a meal and joined them for dinner. It was easier for her to do, since Jackson didn't get home until almost six on band rehearsal days.

The high school band still performed for the school Christmas concert held in mid-December. It had always been a big deal, and considering the twice-a-week after-school rehearsals, they should be in good shape by then. She looked forward to going and maybe even taking the girls with her, if it was okay with Jackson.

"Zoe, do you want to help me set the table?" Maddie asked.

"Sure." Zoe tidied up her books and set them on the back counter. Then she scooped up the quarters, dimes and nickels, and handed them to Maddie. "Thanks for letting me use these."

"Of course." Maddie pocketed the change, then wiped off the table with a fresh dishcloth.

Zoe had homework and she'd been sitting at the kitchen table completing coin identification and time-telling worksheets. Maddie had offered help by giving her real examples of the coins she had to identify. The smart little girl had gotten them all right.

They both set out plates and silverware while Dora helped with folding napkins. They were a bit crooked and messy, but the little one loved to help. Anything Zoe did, Dora wanted to join in.

"Good job, Dora." Maddie smiled. "Shall we count them out together as you place them under the knives?"

"Yup." Dora grinned at her, stealing her heart all over again.

Maddie started. "One."

Dora continued. "Two, fwee, four."

"Very good."

"I can count to ten," the four-year-old bragged.

Maddie laughed. "I know. Your preschool teacher said you were doing great with your numbers."

"Yup." Dora didn't talk a whole lot, and unfortunately, she still sucked on her two fingers.

Was that something she'd outgrow, or should Maddie press Jackson about doing more to deter the habit? It wasn't her place to push, but still. She turned the oven down to warm and glanced at the clock. Jackson would be home soon.

Dinner was a simple one of meat loaf and baked potatoes, green beans and salad. For dessert, Maddie had made a pumpkin pie. She looked forward to sharing meals with the Taylors because it made her feel like part of their family. Part of a *complete* family.

Growing up, Maddie had had her mom, her grandfather and Pearl. It was better than some, but the absence of her father had stung. He hadn't loved her enough to stay in touch and that had left a hole in her life. One she'd tried to fill with Stan. Big mistake.

Those song lyrics whispered through her thoughts yet again. *Hearts get broken.* She'd had her heart broken enough. She'd tried to coax Stan to attend church with her, to no avail. Maddie had grown used to hanging in the background when Stan was home. It was like she hid from her marriage—her life too. Dare she take the risk with Jackson? She wished she knew.

"Is Pearl going to eat wif us?" Dora asked.

"No. We fed her before we came over, remember?" Maddie chuckled. She couldn't imagine Jackson wanting Pearl in the kitchen with them. One more reason to be careful. Any man she got involved with must love parrots. Pearl went with her. End of discussion.

Zoe pointed at her chest. "I fed her."

Maddie smiled. "Yes. Zoe fed her chop. Pearl's probably chillin' in her cage."

"Can she come over?" Dora asked.

Jackson's youngest had become very friendly with the parrot. Pearl liked climbing into Dora' lap, which was the funniest thing. Maddie had never seen Pearl do that with anyone before. It was as if the bird knew Dora was practically a baby and met Dora on a child's level. Her parrot loved both girls. And Maddie did too.

The side door opened. "Something smells amazing."

*Jackson.*

Maddie's heart did somersaults. She looked up just as he walked into the kitchen. His short hair was wind-blown, a lock of it sticking straight up and begging her to smooth it back into place.

"Hi," she said.

"Hi." His voice practically purred. "What's for dinner?"

"Meat loaf." Maddie busied herself at the sink washing her hands.

"Nice. I'll wash up and be back in a sec." Jackson bent down to give both Dora and Zoe hugs. "How are my girls today?"

"Maddie helped me with my homework," Zoe said.

"Great." He looked at her. "Thank you."

Maddie shrugged.

"Now we'll have plenty of time later tonight for piano lessons."

Zoe threw back her head and slumped her shoulders. "Do we have to?"

Jackson shook his head. "I can't believe my daughter doesn't love the piano. Who are you, child?"

Zoe laughed. "Mom liked it when you and her played, didn't she, Dad?"

Jackson's expression changed to one of haunted remorse. "Yeah, honey. She sure did."

Maddie could hardly breathe. She didn't want to interrupt their moment. Such a sad situation, and yet they were okay. They seemed to be healing from their loss, and reminiscing was part of that. Loved ones lived on in cherished memories.

They lived in bad memories too. How did Jackson battle those? Did the piano help? Maddie savored hearing Jackson playing the piano from her house. It was a faint sound, but sometimes she'd hear it more clearly late at night when the wind was still and the street quiet.

He must miss his wife terribly. Another reason to keep her distance. Maddie didn't want to be anyone's rebound romance.

"I'll wash up." Jackson's gaze connected with hers.

She nodded, trying to decipher the depth of his grief in his blue eyes. He looked lonely. Like her. She couldn't comfort him because she'd take more than she could give. Maddie needed a strong embrace, but she feared what that might cost her. Much too dangerous.

"Okay, girls, let's wash our hands too." Shifting gears, she guided Zoe and Dora to the kitchen sink, since Jackson had gone to the powder room.

In minutes, they were seated at the table, and Maddie said a quick blessing over the food. She stood to slice the meat loaf and asked Jackson about his day. "So, how was rehearsal? Is the band ready for the Christmas concert?"

Jackson sliced a potato in half for each girl, then cut one for his plate. He loaded each with butter and sour cream. "We're focusing on the Veterans Day Program right now."

Maddie stopped midslice. "Veterans Day?"

"Yeah, you know, the Veterans Day Program. It's this Saturday and you're a special award recipient. I saw your name on the schedule."

She felt her muscles clench and her vision might have momentarily blurred. She'd never considered that the high school band would be playing this Saturday. But of course they would. And Jackson would finally see her for the fraud she was.

"Everything okay?" he asked.

She served a small slice of meat loaf to Dora and then to Zoe. "Yes. Fine. Everything is just fine."

But it wasn't. Jackson was going to watch her receive an award for Stan. She'd fool them all, acting the part of a grieving widow. But it felt even more like a lie when faced with delivering her speech in front of Jackson. She might fall apart onstage. And then what? Could she explain the nature of her marriage to a man who'd loved his wife? Jackson would never understand.

Maddie considered the pastor's words about confession as a way to forgiveness. Would she finally be free if she told Jackson what she'd said to Stan the night before he'd left? Even if such a confession might set her free, it could cost her Jackson's regard.

Maddie didn't want to make that trade.

Jackson noticed that Maddie had been quiet through dinner. In fact, she'd seemed withdrawn ever since he'd mentioned the Veterans Day Program. She must be facing a difficult weekend ahead and he'd just reminded her of it. *Good job.*

They had all cleared the table, but Jackson loaded the dishwasher while Maddie packed up the leftovers in plastic containers. The girls escaped to the living room to watch a little TV before piano lessons, then bed.

"Maddie, I want to thank you again for everything you're doing here."

She looked at him, puzzled. "You're paying me—"

He held up his hand. She'd said so before and he realized he didn't like the way it sounded coming from her. "Maybe so, but you're going above and beyond and you're helping the girls heal. I really appreciate it."

She was helping him heal too, but he couldn't admit that. Not yet, anyway, because that might lead into dating territory. If he asked her out only to have her refuse, then what?

"I'm glad this is working out. I truly love those little girls." She quickly looked away and focused on packing the leftovers in the fridge.

A blind man could tell that she loved his girls, and Jackson certainly could see clearly enough. One thing he'd noticed since meeting her was that she kept her grief locked up tight. If he shared a little of his own pain, would she open up and share hers? For whatever reason, her church's grief support group hadn't really helped her. Could he, even if only a little bit? It was worth a shot.

"I didn't tell you why we moved here." He set the tea-kettle on to boil. "Want some hot chocolate?"

"Sure," she said.

He had her attention. "My wife battled depression most of her adult life. When we married, it was manageable. With Zoe, it was too, but after Dora was born, her condition grew worse. Much worse. I don't know why, the doctors didn't know why, but there were times when Delia didn't get out of bed for days."

"I'm so sorry." Maddie slipped into a chair at the table.

He leaned against the sink. "It wasn't easy. I prayed and prayed for her healing and did whatever I could to help her, but it wasn't enough. God let her suffer." He didn't want to go into too much detail that might upset her, so he moved on. "After she overdosed, there were murmurs in the church we attended, stuff about me neglecting Delia's illness, or that I did something to break her heart."

Maddie's eyes grew wide. "That's awful."

He shrugged. "It's amazing how callous people can be, especially the ones you'd expect to give compassion and understanding when needed most. The ones who are supposed to reach out, lash out instead. Needless to say, I stopped going to church, but when those rumors resurfaced and followed Zoe to school this fall, I knew we had to leave."

"So, you took the open position at Pine Middle School."

"For the girls' sake, yes. Zoe is working through her grief pretty well. We talk a lot. Dora? I just don't know. She was only three when Delia died."

The teakettle whistled, so Jackson turned off the gas burner. Maddie stepped right next to him as if contemplating how to give him support or comfort or something.

"Should we make some for Zoe and Dora?" Her voice was low and soft.

"They'd be mad if we didn't." He chuckled, relieved that she played it safe and kept her distance.

Maddie reached for the mugs while he grabbed the container of powdered mix. It was a big one. They often drank hot cocoa before bedtime. Opening the lid, Jackson scooped out the mix and dumped it in each mug, and then Maddie touched his wrist.

He looked up fast.

Her eyes were glassy and wet. "Is there anything I can do to help the girls?"

He covered her hand with his own, but it wasn't enough. His arms itched to pull her close. "You're already doing it, just by being you. They've liked you from the start, Maddie, and maybe it's because they sense your own loss and that comforts them."

She looked down at their joined hands.

"I know this Saturday will be hard for you. I have my parents coming this weekend, so it'll be a little hectic, but anything I can do to help you, just say the word."

"Thank you, but it's something I have to work through on my own," Maddie said.

He watched as her expression changed into one of fortitude and determination before closing up tight.

She pulled her hand away. "I'm merely accepting an award. There's no reason I can't get through it. I'll be fine."

"I'm sure you will, but I'm here just the same."

"I know." Maddie finally looked away and grabbed a spoon.

Jackson poured hot water into the mugs. He grabbed the can of whipped cream from the fridge while Maddie stirred the hot chocolate. Shaking the can first, he sprayed a dollop into each mug.

It made Maddie giggle. "Whoa, that's a lot of cream."

Jackson winked at her. "You should see my banana splits."

"Don't tease me." Maddie looked at him with amusement shining in her blue eyes. Her glasses had slid down her nose again, but she pushed them back in place as if trying to hide behind them.

He smiled, enjoying the light, almost flirty, banter between them. Glancing at her mouth and her perfectly shaped set of lips, he wondered what would happen if he kissed her. Just one taste—but he knew one kiss wouldn't be enough.

Maddie backed up as if reading his thoughts. "Maybe I should take mine to go."

"Why?"

She closed her eyes and tipped her head back just like Zoe dragging her feet over piano practice. "Because it's late."

"Come on, Maddie. Stick around a little while longer. Zoe would love to have you stay for her lesson and I promise to behave." Jackson hoped to lighten her up a little.

She gave him a hint of a smile that said she'd received his message loud and clear. Instead of leaving, Maddie headed for the living room with two mugs in her hands.

\* \* \*

After Zoe's piano lesson and a refill of hot chocolate for all of them, Maddie stood. She really needed to leave before she did something stupid like let Jackson kiss her. He wanted to—she'd seen it in his eyes. "Okay, ladies and gentleman, I had best go home and get Pearl settled in for the night."

"Awwwww, don't go yet," Zoe whined.

"It's time to get ready for bed, Zoe." Jackson rose as well, grabbing the girls' two mugs with one hand.

"Can Maddie tuck us in?"

Maddie felt the quicksand closing in around her. She couldn't bring herself to say no after what these girls had been through. Jackson too. Her heart broke for all of them; it also beat a little too hard for them as well. She was a temporary nanny, not part of their family.

"Please?" Jackson was no help.

"Okay, okay." Maddie gave in to the cheers of two little girls jumping up and down.

"Zoe, go on up with Maddie, and I'll be up in a minute."

"Race ya!" Zoe dashed for the stairs, followed by Dora, trying to keep up.

"Careful." Maddie's caution fell on deaf ears as she made her way through the front foyer to the large staircase.

The front entrance was huge and pretty. She could imagine turning it into a sitting area with a cozy reading nook cut into the decorative wall under the stairs. With the high ceiling, there was lots of potential in this space.

It wasn't her house, and they were not her family.

Talk about a somber reminder not to get too comfortable here. This gig was only short-term. Maddie climbed the stairs, hearing sounds of the girls squealing as they opened dresser drawers. Would they even sleep after getting so riled up?

The upstairs had a big open hallway with a full bathroom, a linen closet and what looked like three bedrooms. The girls shared the room facing the backyard. She stepped in as they were slipping into jammies.

"Here, Dora, let me help you." The little one couldn't get her feet into the footed bottoms of her pj's.

"I gotta go to the bafroom."

"Go ahead. I'll be here when you get back." Maddie sat on Dora's twin bed.

"Zoe, go in and help your sister brush her teeth, and make sure you both use the potty and wash your hands." Jackson had entered their room.

"Okay." Zoe dashed out.

He stooped to pick up the clothes on the floor and tossed them in the wicker hamper.

Maddie watched him, feeling exposed and inadequate. Helping the girls with their nightly routine was an intimate act of a family member. She didn't belong here, but couldn't for the life of her refuse, because deep down, she wanted to belong.

Maddie wanted to belong with *him* and that was scary.

She switched gears. "Do you read them a story?"

"Sometimes." Jackson checked his watch. "But it's up to you."

Dora came in and climbed up onto her bed. "Tuck me in?"

Maddie pulled the blankets back for her to wiggle under. Then she folded them up over her belly. "How's that?"

Dora nodded. "Good."

Zoe came in next and climbed into her bed. She pulled

a stuffed elephant that wore a dress into her arms. "Can you read us a story?"

"Sure." Maddie grabbed one of the books on the table between the two beds and started reading. "'There once was a prince who wished to marry a princess…'"

Maddie was acutely aware of Jackson when he sat across from her on Zoe's bed. Although he'd probably read this story a million times, he listened to her read it with a rapt expression on his face. It nearly unnerved her, but she kept telling the short and sweet tale of a princess who slept on a pea. No Romeo and Juliet tales were in that stack of books—too tragic.

Zoe giggled at the part about the queen placing mattress upon mattress.

"And they lived happily ever after even though they ate the pea." Maddie ended the story with her own twist.

Zoe smiled. "They didn't eat the pea."

Maddie smiled back. "They might have."

Jackson leaned down and kissed his oldest daughter on the forehead. "Okay, lights out. Dora's almost asleep."

Maddie glanced at the youngest. Sure enough, her eyes drooped. She'd never seen a kid who could fall asleep so fast, but then, Maddie wasn't around too many children. She stood and got out of the way so Jackson could kiss Dora's head.

He did so and then turned off the bedside light. A night-light gleamed from the opposite wall.

"Wait." Zoe reached out her hand. "Maddie, will you help me say my prayers?"

Maddie's heart skipped a beat. She looked to Jackson for his reaction. He nodded for her to go ahead, but even in the low light, she could see his jaw clenched tight. So, he was still mad at God. She had to step carefully here.

She reached for Zoe's hand and held Dora's wrist while she knelt in between both girls' beds. "Go ahead."

"God bless Mommy and Daddy and give us a good night sleep."

"Amen." Maddie squeezed Zoe's hand, but the girl didn't let go.

"And please help Daddy pray again. Amen." Zoe let go then.

"Good night, girls," Maddie whispered as she followed Jackson out of the room.

He looked like he'd been slapped.

When they were headed down the stairs, Maddie worked up the courage to ask, "Did you hear that?"

He nodded.

Silently, they walked through the living room and reached the side entrance, where Maddie stopped. It was time for her to go, but she couldn't just yet. "What happened to your relationship with God?"

"I stopped praying because He didn't answer my prayers to heal my wife." Jackson's blue eyes were dark with fury and hurt.

Maddie couldn't fault him. Not really. Her heart hurt. For him and for her. What might her marriage have been like had Stan loved her with an ounce of how Jackson had loved his wife? Marrying Stan wasn't God's fault. It was hers and hers alone. She'd been warned that they were too young, but she hadn't listened.

Wanting to soothe Jackson's anger if she could, Maddie offered up the first thing that came to her mind. "What if God was in the process of healing your wife but didn't get the chance here, on earth?"

He looked at her, through her, and then his face seemed to lighten. "I never thought of it in that way."

"God answers prayer, just not always in our time

frame or by our rules." Maddie repeated what she'd heard Erica Laine say about the death of her husband. It rang true then and now.

"How'd you keep your faith after going through such loss?"

"Faith was the only thing I had." She could dodge his earnest question and yet she didn't want to mislead him into thinking she'd been happy. "My marriage wasn't a good one. Stan was possessive and downright mean at times. He never hit me, but once he choked me pretty good just to prove he had control."

Jackson's eyes widened. "Why'd you stay with him?"

Shame filled her. Maybe she shouldn't have been so blunt, but Maddie couldn't stop the honest answers from pouring out. "I left him once. He found out where I stayed, broke in quietly and stole Pearl while I slept. He left a note that he'd kill her if I didn't return. I knew he'd make good on that threat no matter where I went or how far, so I went back and stayed."

"Why didn't you report him?" Jackson looked horrified.

"He was a decorated soldier. No MP would do anything under threat to a pet parrot. I promised my dying grandfather I'd take care of Pearl for the rest of her lifetime and that's what I aim to do. Stan was gone most of the time on deployment, so I got by on my own just fine." Maddie sniffed bitterly. It had been a lonely existence tiptoeing her way through a rough marriage.

Jackson reached for her hands and gave them a squeeze. "I'm sorry."

"I guess I'm more like my mom than I thought—really bad taste in men. I'm glad he's gone, and that's an unforgivable response. I keep praying for forgiveness, but..."

She shrugged as she stared at their clasped hands. Was Jackson another bad choice waiting to happen?

"That relief is natural, considering what you went through." Jackson let go in order to tip up her chin, so she'd look him in the eyes. "I had guilt over my relief after Delia's death too. Maddie, I understand that struggle. I never knew what I'd come home to. Dora probably won't remember the worst times—she was just a toddler—but Zoe will. Zoe had to walk on eggshells because her mother could fall apart with little provocation."

Maddie felt her eyes burn. She knew all about walking on eggshells. Why was life so unfair?

"God forgave you, Maddie. It's your turn to forgive yourself." He cupped her face with his hand, and his thumb traced a line across her cheek until he brushed the top of her upper lip.

Her skin warmed beneath his touch. "It's late. I need to head home."

"Okay, but, Maddie—" his voice sounded hoarse "—I'd really like to kiss you good-night."

She'd like that too. More than anything.

At her hesitation, Jackson lifted his hands in surrender. "Just say the word and I'll back off."

Maddie didn't want to form those words, so she simply stared at him and waited.

Jackson reached up and removed her glasses. "Is this okay?"

*No, it's not.*

She felt like he could see straight down into her soul and the secrets she kept there. Would he still want to kiss her if he knew what she'd said to Stan? She couldn't even use the heat of the argument as an excuse because she'd meant every single word.

"You're a beautiful woman, Maddie. Inside and out."

*I'm not.*

And then his lips touched hers and Maddie closed her eyes. So gentle was his attention, she had to grip his forearms to keep herself upright. She finally responded and kissed him back, but that opened up another basket of concerns when he deepened the kiss—turning her inside out.

*What am I doing?*

Maddie had never been so thoroughly kissed in her life. Now she knew what she'd been missing all those years with Stan, even the halfway decent ones. She'd never felt this cherished or safe, even while inching toward a precipice she'd better back away from before she plunged headfirst over the edge.

But Jackson was the one who pulled back, saving them from the edge.

He gave her the softest of smiles. "Good night, Maddie. Sleep tight."

She wrapped her arms around herself to keep from reaching for him and watched as he held out her glasses. She took them from his fingertips without looking away. "Good night, Jackson."

She put her glasses firmly back in place like a shield. As she looked through the lenses, there was her Romeo focused more clearly, holding her coat open for her.

She slipped into it. "Thanks."

He gave her shoulders a quick squeeze. "You're welcome. See you tomorrow."

Maddie nodded and slipped out the door. She ran for her house, but she couldn't outrun the regret that had morphed into dread by the time she opened her front door.

What if she said the wrong thing during her acceptance speech? Jackson would see her for the fraud she really was. And who would want a liar watching his girls?

# Chapter Ten

Two days later, Jackson couldn't shake the feeling that he'd messed up by kissing Maddie. The fact that she'd kissed him back seemed moot. As soon as he'd come home yesterday, she'd darted out the door with the excuse that she had a meeting in Marquette about selling her hat-and-mitten sets. He hadn't had a chance to talk with her alone.

Maybe tonight, they'd talk. What he'd say, he had no idea. All he knew was that he shouldn't have kissed her. It was too soon for both of them. Her deer-in-the-headlights expression yesterday may have confirmed that. And he was her employer too, which added to the inappropriateness of it all.

Still, kissing Maddie had felt like part of him that had been missing for a long time had finally been found. The way she'd trembled had made him pull back, and that re-action worried him still. Maddie had been deeply hurt in her marriage, so it was no wonder she was afraid.

In fact, the two men who were supposed to love and protect her had failed. First her father and then her husband. Jackson refused to be added to that list. He shouldn't press into a relationship neither were ready for. No matter how much he wanted to wipe away Maddie's hurt, the risks might be too great—for her, for him and for his girls.

He pulled into his driveway and cut the engine. Running a hand through his hair, he figured he'd take his cues from Maddie. If she was open to talking, then they'd talk. If not, they wouldn't.

He got out into cold drizzle and hurried inside. The tantalizing aroma of something really good hit his senses. Had she used the pork chops he'd left in the fridge? Whatever it was smelled marvelous.

"Hi, Daddy." Zoe crashed into him with a hug.

"You're going to get all wet." His jacket dripped.

"I don't care." She grinned up at him, not letting go.

He grinned back. "Have a good day?"

"Yes."

He looked beyond his daughter into the kitchen. Maddie was whipping something on the stove. Her hair had been pulled into a long braid that hung down to the middle of her back. His pulse picked up speed.

She turned, caught him watching her and then looked away. "Dinner is almost ready."

"No hurry." He disentangled Zoe and pulled off his jacket, which he then hung up.

"I have to leave right after." She still wouldn't look at him.

So, there was the cue he'd wanted. No talking tonight. "What's up?"

"I have to go over to my mom's. She wants to help me with my...speech." Her voice cracked.

He stepped into the kitchen with Zoe still hanging on him, standing on his feet. "Maddie, is everything okay?"

She looked at him then, just barely before focusing back on the pillows of mashed potatoes she'd made. "Yes. Why?"

*For starters, you won't look me in the eye.*

Had he scared her that much with just one kiss? "Zoe, will you let go, please? Where's your sister?"

"Asleep on the couch," Maddie and Zoe both chorused.

"Better wake her up or she won't sleep tonight." Jackson winked at his daughter who then ran to do the deed. Dora was funny when she first woke up, like she didn't know where she was for a few seconds.

With Zoe gone, Jackson struggled with whether to bring up the other night but then decided against it. He didn't want to be rushed or pressured. And maybe he should just let it go. Maddie might not welcome his romantic attempts and was simply too kind to tell him.

She'd kissed him back, sure, but he'd had to coax her. When she'd finally opened up... The clanging rattle of a sauce pot lid obliterated his thoughts.

Maddie picked up the dropped top and covered up the mashed potatoes and then opened the oven.

"What did you make?" The fragrance coming out of the oven was beyond amazing. This woman could really cook, and he could get used to this real fast.

"Cherry-and-mushroom-stuffed pork chops."

"Wow. Anything I can do?" Jackson noticed that the table had already been set and glasses were filled with ice water. Maddie had gotten them into the habit of drinking water with dinner on Tuesdays and Thursdays instead of pop or milk.

"Nope. I think we're all set." Maddie pulled out the pan of pork chops and set them on the stove top.

Jackson couldn't help but hover and breathe deep. It took every inch of his willpower not to wrap his arms around Maddie's waist and nuzzle her neck. He liked having her here for dinner. No, more than that, he didn't like saying good-night to her anymore.

Zoe and a sleepy Dora stepped into the kitchen, and Zoe slipped into her seat. "We washed our hands."

Dora climbed into her booster seat. "Me too."

"I better wash mine." Jackson went for the sink, but he was acutely aware of Maddie moving around his kitchen like she belonged here. He wanted her to belong here for always and that was a scary thought by itself. Was he ready? Was Maddie? They may have simply connected out of sheer loneliness, but it sure felt like more than that. Way more.

She retrieved a bowl of what looked like Waldorf salad from the fridge and set it on the table. "I figured we could fill the plates at the stove since everything is so hot."

He stepped forward. "Sounds good."

She went to grab a plate the same time he did and they did an awkward dance in the middle of the kitchen. She laughed and gestured with her hand. "You go first."

The girls giggled too.

"I'll get Zoe's if you want to fill Dora's plate," Jackson offered.

Maddie nodded, but she seemed a little jumpy. Anxious even.

When all the plates were filled and they were seated, Jackson looked at Maddie. "Would you like to say a blessing?"

"Sure." She bowed her head.

"We should hold hands." Zoe reached for his and Dora's. Jackson reached for Maddie's, conscious of the softness of her skin. Again, he felt her tremble, so he gave her hand an encouraging squeeze. What was going on inside her head? He wished he knew.

Maddie gave a quick prayer of thanks and pulled her hand away without an answering squeeze or gesture.

He knew rejection when he saw it, and Maddie had

done just that. She wasn't interested in a romantic relationship. And that was okay, he supposed, for now. He'd assure her that he valued her friendship and hope no harm was done. He'd apologize for making her uncomfortable, since she'd reminded him more than once that he was her employer. He'd ask for her forgiveness. Maybe this weekend while his parents were here, he could ask her to dinner or to go for a drive so they could talk privately.

He took a bite of the pork chop that was so tender, it literally melted in his mouth, but the delicious taste was lost on him. He didn't want to be just friends with Maddie. Not by a long shot.

Maddie was a mess. Between her growing feelings for Jackson and the fear that she'd say the wrong thing in her acceptance speech, Maddie couldn't seem to concentrate. Sitting at her mom's kitchen table with a cup of tea and a plate of homemade sugar cookies, she crumpled up yet another piece of paper. She couldn't for the life of her write a few good sentences about Stan. Everything felt like a lie. With the exception of his prowess as a soldier and his desire to serve his country.

"Just speak from your heart," her mother encouraged.

That might be disastrous. Maddie had to keep her heart out of it. That wounded organ had hardened considerably toward her late husband.

Her mother's husband was watching football in the living room. The TV blared, but her mother didn't ask him to turn the volume down.

Maddie closed her eyes against the pounding in her head. If she spoke from the heart, she'd say something she'd regret. Maddie didn't want to tarnish her in-laws' memory of their son. That wouldn't be fair to them. Or her. What could she possibly gain by tearing down Stan even though she wanted to set the record straight?

She felt her mom's hand on her shoulder. "Maddie, are you okay?"

*No.*

"I'm just nervous about Saturday. I'm not really comfortable speaking in public." She looked at her mom, tempted to tell her what it had been like being married to Stan, but not with Paul in the house. He reminded her too much of her late husband. Paul was big, loud and overbearing too.

"It doesn't have to be a long speech."

"Stan's parents are coming, so it has to be good. This is more for them than me." That was the truth.

Her mom tipped her head, looking as if she was trying to put the pieces together, but couldn't. "Why do you say that?"

Maddie held her mother's gaze, willing her to understand, but then, what was the point? It'd only make her mother feel bad if she knew the truth about the last five years.

Maddie shrugged. "He was their son."

"But your husband."

Maddie rued the day she'd made that happen. If only she had listened. If they'd dated longer, maybe Maddie would have seen the controlling side of Stan.

Just then, Paul entered the kitchen. "Got any more chips and dip?"

Her mother hurried to ply her husband with snacks and send him back into the living room.

"You know what, Mom? I think I'm going to go." Maddie stood and grabbed her purse. If for no other reason than to escape the volume of the TV.

Her mom grabbed her hand. "Honey, I'm sorry. I thought I could help."

Maddie smiled, not wanting her mother to worry. "Some things a girl just has to do on her own."

Her mother nodded.

"Touchdown!" Paul yelled from the living room. "Shelly, come see this."

"Not now—Maddie is leaving." Her mother rolled her eyes. "Come on. I'll walk you out."

"If you need to go—"

Her mother placed a finger on Maddie's lips to shush her. "I don't."

Paul peeked his head into the kitchen and smiled sheepishly. "'Bye, Maddie."

Surprised that Paul looked like a kid caught with his hand in the cookie jar, Maddie smiled back and slipped into her coat. Maybe she was wrong about him. She prayed that she was, for her mother's sake. "'Bye, Paul."

Out on the porch, her mother turned and gave her a hug. "I'll pick you up Saturday morning, okay?"

"That would be great. Thank you." Driving and then finding a place to park would be one less thing to worry about.

"I meant to ask how your nanny job is going," her mother said.

Maddie rubbed her mom's arm. "It's good. Go inside or you'll freeze."

"You can tell me all about it Saturday. Love you," her mom called out.

"Love you too." Maddie waved and slipped into her car. She started the engine, letting it warm up before she backed out. Her mother stood on the front porch, watching until she was on the road, before going inside and turning off the porch light.

Maddie had dodged a bullet, so to speak. She might be able to hold back her life with Stan from her mom, but she wasn't sure she could hide her growing feelings for Jackson if asked.

Tonight had been agony seeing the apology hovering in Jackson's eyes. No doubt, he regretted the kiss they'd shared and was on the brink of saying so. She hadn't wanted to hear it. Not now, not ever.

It didn't take long before she pulled into her own driveway. Shutting off the car, she got out and closed the door quietly. She couldn't help but glance toward Jackson's house. Sure enough, he stood at the kitchen sink with soft light shining from behind him. Could she get in the house before he saw her?

Too late. He not only spotted her, but raised his finger in a gesture to have her wait.

Maddie looked up into the clear, moonless sky and the millions of stars scattered like glitter. She released a deep breath that made a frosty puff in front of her. They were in for a really cold night. A heavy frost kind of night. Pulling the collar of her coat close, she walked toward the Taylors' side porch.

Jackson came out. "Hey, how'd you do with your speech?"

"Horribly."

He chuckled. "Can I help?"

She shook her head. "No. But thank you for offering."

"You're welcome. Look, Maddie—"

"The girls?"

"In bed. I wanted—"

Maddie interrupted again to keep from hearing that apology. "Did you pray with them?"

His face softened. "Yes. I knelt down while Zoe said her prayers."

Maddie smiled. He hadn't said that he prayed too, but at least he went through the motion for his girls. Besides, Jackson was too good a man to stay mad at God forever. He'd make his way back. It was what she'd been praying for.

He stepped closer. "Look, about the other night—"

Maddie took a step back. "If you're going to apologize, please don't."

His eyes widened. "You've been so distant, I thought, well, I thought you'd regretted what happened between us."

Oh, why'd she say anything? "I'm just nervous about Saturday."

"Your speech?" He took another step toward her.

"I feel like such a liar."

Jackson cupped her cheek. "Keep it general and give thanks to those who serve, and you'll do fine."

"I'll try." She bit her lip, waiting for what came next.

He tucked a strand of her hair behind her ear. "I have to be there early, but you can ride with me if you'd like. My parents are bringing the girls."

"My mom is picking me up." Maddie looked into his eyes and saw nothing but kindness there.

He really did care. Maybe he was right and it'd be okay. Given what she'd told him, maybe he'd understand why she'd said those awful words to Stan. If only she'd rally the courage to tell him. Maybe someday, they could have a future together. She'd be careful and take her time—make sure Jackson was the kind of man she could trust.

She clenched her jaw. How on earth would she know for sure?

"Okay." He leaned closer and kissed her forehead. "Good night, Maddie."

"Good night." Maddie smiled to cover the disappointment surging through her.

*Just a kiss on the forehead?*

And then it dawned on her. Was it too soon for him to get involved? He'd only been widowed twelve months. Maybe Jackson was afraid of the kiss they'd shared and that was why he'd applied the brakes.

She walked into her house, threw her purse on the floor and hung up her coat. "Hey, Pearl."

"Idiot!" The parrot ruffled her feathers and screeched like she was mad that Maddie had been gone all evening.

"You're right on target with that one." Maddie threw herself on the couch.

She *was* an idiot for hoping she might get a second chance at love.

The next day, Jackson had texted Maddie that she didn't need to pick up Dora since his parents were coming earlier than expected and would pick her up from preschool. He'd also invited Maddie to join them for dinner—they were going out for pizza.

He'd been disappointed when she'd texted back that she needed to prepare for her acceptance speech. He wasn't sure why this speech gave her such grief, but whatever. He didn't want to press her, but he had wanted her to meet his parents. That would have to wait until tomorrow.

After they met her, Jackson planned on asking his parents to watch the girls while he took Maddie out for dinner tomorrow night. They needed to talk now more than ever, especially after Maddie had no remorse about the kiss they'd shared. That boded well for more. If Maddie was open to the idea, he'd like them to start dating. They needed to get to know each other better before they exchanged too many more kisses.

*Only fools rush in.*

He'd held himself in check last night. He'd been so close to inviting Maddie in for a cup of hot chocolate by the fire and that would not have been wise with the girls already in bed. He needed to take this relationship slowly and with care. Not only for his and Maddie's sakes, but he didn't want his girls getting hurt, either.

Jackson focused on getting his girls into their coats, hats and mittens so they could go to dinner. He chuckled when he realized his mother hadn't noticed that the girls' woolens were made from her gifted sweaters. He'd tell her when he had to and not a moment before.

"What's so funny?" his mom asked.

"Not a thing." Jackson looked around. "Are we ready?"

"Yes." Zoe was already opening the door.

They headed for the car and the pizza joint that awaited. Jackson spotted Maddie's Subaru parked in her driveway.

Zoe pulled on his coat, looking up at him. "Where's Maddie?"

"She's busy getting her speech ready for tomorrow." Jackson opened the back door of his Subaru. He'd moved the girls' car seats to the third row to make room for his parents and Maddie, if she'd have joined them.

"But I want her to come with us." Zoe climbed in.

"I know, honey. I do too, but she's busy." Jackson glanced at Maddie's house. The lights were on, giving a warm, yellow glow to the windows.

Dora followed her sister, climbing into the booster seat. Once buckled in, she looked up at him with a trembling bottom lip. "I miss Maddie."

"You'll see her tomorrow," Jackson assured her.

It had only been one day without Maddie, yet his youngest was homesick for her. She'd become attached to their pretty neighbor, which was a good thing and definitely the reason to approach this attraction between him and Maddie with care. Jackson was looking toward the future, yet he had to be sure about their present first.

He slid behind the wheel, while his father climbed into the passenger seat and his mom sat in one of the two back captain's chairs. He checked his rearview mirror. "Everyone ready?"

"Yes!" Zoe yelled.

"Me too," Dora chimed in, her longing for Maddie forgotten.

He smiled, catching Dora's gaze. Kids could switch gears so fast.

As he backed out of the driveway, he glanced quickly again at Maddie's house. Was she truly struggling over her speech? Considering what she'd shared about Stan, he could understand the hurdle she had to jump in order to write a good acceptance speech.

Considering her nervousness over the shrunken sweaters, Jackson wondered if Maddie was afraid to face his mother. He guessed that might be true. Maybe Maddie was afraid of confrontation. He couldn't blame her. Sometimes, he feared his mother too, and that thought made him laugh again.

"Now what's so funny?" his mother asked.

He caught his mother's stern gaze in the rearview mirror and turned his amusement into a cough. "Nothing."

The drive into town was short, and when they were finally seated and their pizza order given, his mother leaned toward him. "The girls sure love this woman you have watching them. Zoe was telling me all about her. Weren't you, Zoe?"

His oldest nodded but didn't look up from the paper she colored. Both girls had been given crayons and activity sheets while they waited for their food.

"Yeah, Maddie's great with them."

His mother nodded. "Then you don't really need day-care for Dora."

He'd thought about that. It was another option he'd have to discuss with Maddie. "She might have other plans, since originally this was a temporary arrangement."

"What plans could she have if she doesn't work?" His mother sipped her cola through a straw.

Jackson forced his tone to remain even. "She makes things. Clothes and hat-and-mitten sets."

"She made ours," Zoe added.

"She did?" His mom grabbed Zoe's hat from inside his daughter's coat sleeve and inspected it. "Very nice."

Jackson held his breath for a minute, but his mom hadn't noticed the pattern as her gifted sweater. He wasn't about to fess up now. "She recently met with a store in Marquette about selling her stuff."

His mother's eyebrows rose. "So, she's like a designer?"

"I don't know, Mom. She likes to sew." His mother had always been too interested in the details. Maybe he was too laid-back, thinking things would simply work out. They hadn't with Delia.

"Well, I look forward to meeting her."

"Tomorrow, Mom."

Jackson didn't care for the protective gleam in his mom's eyes, as if Maddie had to pass her inspection. Really, he was a grown man who could make decisions for himself and his girls. He wasn't the same impulsive man who'd met and married Delia within three months. He was wiser now, more cautious.

Only fools rushed in, and Jackson was no fool.

## Chapter Eleven

Maddie walked into the Pine High School auditorium and stepped back in time. Deep burgundy velvet drapes still framed the stage. The same color covered the theater-style seats that were a little more worn than they used to be. She spotted the Pine Bobcats banner in the school colors of burgundy and white. It still hung on the wall to the left of the stage. Her high school hadn't changed much.

She had, though. Maybe too much. This was supposed to feel like home, but it didn't. In fact, she wanted to turn tail and run far away. Maddie clutched her purse a little closer, her stomach roiling. Her speech note cards were tucked safely in the outside pocket, along with the program schedule, so that she could grab them quickly.

"I'll hang up our coats backstage. You look very nice, by the way."

"Thanks, Mom." Maddie had chosen her clothes with care. Nothing too complicated or patterned. A simple gray skirt with a matching tunic-style sweater looked serious, but comfortable. She'd added some color with red boots.

She watched her mother climb the steps leading to the stage, and then she disappeared behind the curtain. Although part of the Ladies Auxiliary, Maddie's mom had only worked on organizing this event. She wasn't part of the presentation, so she'd sit in the audience with her fellow volunteers.

A row of chairs had been set up onstage, along with a podium. Maddie would be sitting in that row, along with other presenters and speakers. A couple of huge American flags hung in the back and a large patriotic floral arrangement stood at the front of the stage. Red-white-and-blue flags were tucked in between red carnations and white gladiolas.

She could hear the students warming up in the band room. They wouldn't file in and take their places in the orchestra pit until just before the program started.

Nerves skittered down her spine, so Maddie closed her eyes and prayed for strength. She really didn't want to mess this up.

"Maddie!"

She opened her eyes and spotted Zoe running down the aisle toward her. Dora wasn't far behind, the four-year-old's smile a mile wide. "Hi, Zoe. Hi, Dora."

An older couple followed. No doubt, they were Jackson's parents. Maddie got a good look at them as they approached. Jackson resembled his mother a lot, while his sister, Melanie, looked more like their dad. They were a nice-looking family.

Maddie opened her arms and hugged both girls, reveling in their little-girl scents of dryer sheet–scented clothes and maple syrup. "You must have had pancakes this morning."

"Waffles," Dora said with a giggle.

Even though it had only been one day, Maddie had missed them. She straightened and approached their grandparents. "Hello, I'm Maddie Williams."

"We've heard a lot about you." Jackson's mother held

out her hand. "I'm Sue Taylor, and this is my husband, Glen."

"Nice to meet you both." She shook their hands.

"Daddy's going to conduct the band." Zoe bounced up and down.

"I know. I look forward to hearing them play." Maddie would be able to watch Jackson easily enough from the stage. He'd see her too. If she fell apart, he'd see it. He'd see it all. She wasn't going to fall apart.

Dora looked around the vast place, her fingers in her mouth.

Jackson's mom pulled Dora's fingers free. "Dora, stop that."

Maddie's defensive hackles went up. That was one way of reacting to Dora's bad habit, but Maddie didn't think it was the best way. She made eye contact with Dora and gave her a smile.

Dora smiled, then stuck her fingers back in her mouth. *Oh boy.*

Jackson's mom didn't seem to notice.

"Will you sit with us?" Zoe asked.

"No, honey. I have to sit on the stage."

The seven-year-old threw her head back. "Awwwww, no fair."

*It sure isn't.*

"I understand your husband passed away this year and you're accepting an award on his behalf. I am very sorry." Mrs. Taylor's words were warm enough, but her gaze seemed cool.

Maddie got the distinct impression that Jackson's mom had sized her up and found her lacking. Maddie brushed her fingers through Dora's curls as the little girl leaned into her, fingers still firmly in her mouth. Maddie gently pulled them out, before Sue Taylor did. "Yes, thank you."

"What branch of military?" Jackson's dad asked.

"Marines." Maddie was used to answering that question.

Jackson's dad looked like he wanted to say something else, but his wife nudged him.

"We better get to our seats. It's filling up fast." Sue Taylor held out her hands for the girls to take. Zoe took her grandmother's hand, but Dora hesitated.

Dora leaned even closer against Maddie's legs. "I wanna sit wif Maddie."

"You can't, Dora. Miss Maddie is part of the program," Sue said in a clipped voice. Jackson's mom seemed very matter-of-fact, while her husband appeared to be laid-back.

Maddie bent down and whispered, "Go with your grandma, Dora. I'll see you a little later, but you can watch me from your seat."

Dora nodded and finally took her grandmother's hand. Zoe draped her arm around her little sister. "You can sit next to me."

Maddie wished she could go with them and sit this one out as she watched Zoe and Dora walk away.

"Who was that?" Her mother stood next to her.

Maddie hadn't even heard her mother's approach. "Those are the two little girls I watch and their grandparents."

"I just missed meeting them." Her mother's regret sounded real.

"I'll introduce you afterward." Maddie watched until the Taylors were seated in a middle row toward the end.

"You better get up there onstage." Her mom nudged her.

The auditorium was filling up fast, and most of the presenters were already in their seats onstage. Maddie blew out her breath. "Okay."

Her mother gave her elbow a quick squeeze. "It'll be okay. Just remember this is for Stan."

Maddie nodded, but that didn't help.

Every time she thought of Stan, she wanted to rant about what a terrible man he'd been to her. Straightening her shoulders, she marched up the steps and took a seat—the one with her name written on a sticker attached to the floor. Staring out over the sea of faces, she shivered. She hadn't anticipated this many people attending.

The band members entered, shuffling softly in a single file. A quiet entrance had always been the way of the Pine Bobcat Band Ensemble, and it appeared Jackson would continue that tradition. They settled into their places in the pit area. All were dressed in somber black, even Jackson. He looked up at that moment and caught her gaze, giving her an encouraging wink.

Maddie gave him a nod. She didn't think a bright smile in return would be appropriate.

Jackson raised his baton and the band started to play "America the Beautiful."

Maddie enjoyed watching him get into the music, pointing to the brass section to increase their sound and then using his other hand to bring in the crash of cymbals. And then lowering his hand to soften the volume. It was great, and Jackson was wonderful at conducting.

She spotted Stan's parents slipping into a side row in the audience just as the mayor of Pine took to the podium to welcome everyone and invite all to stand and sing the chorus of "My Country 'Tis of Thee."

After they sat back down, Maddie pulled the note cards and schedule out of the side pocket of her purse and held them in her lap. Waiting.

As the program progressed, Maddie's nerves only grew.

What if she let it slip that she didn't deserve this award because she'd wanted her husband to die? What then?

An honorary video had been made with photos of several of the Pine community's fallen from years past up to current time. Jackson's band played "A Salute to US Forces" softly during the video and then stopped when Stan's picture, the last one to die, looked out from the screen. His face taunted her. She could hear him yelling at her that his death was her fault.

Maddie refocused on the program. Stan's picture was her cue that she'd soon be called to accept the award.

After a brief introduction, the mayor called her name and stepped back.

*This is it.*

Maddie gripped her note cards, stood and approached the podium. "Hello."

The audience echoed her greeting back with warmth.

She glanced at Jackson.

He gave her a warm, encouraging smile.

Taking a deep breath, Maddie set her note cards on the stand in front of her, in case she needed them. "Thank you for coming today. I'm grateful that my in-laws are here, because Stan would have liked this very much."

She paused, letting that truth sink in. Despite Stan's faults, he'd loved serving his country. She could do this. Taking a deep breath, she went on. "Forgive me for being nervous, as that doesn't do those who have served any justice. For they learned to overcome far more than mere nerves..."

It wasn't a long speech, but Maddie's voice grew stronger as she spoke. She'd thought of her grandfather's service when she'd written these words. He'd fought in Vietnam, and it wasn't something he liked to speak about, even though she'd asked time and again what it had been like. He'd been a Marine as well.

Maddie wrapped up by saying, "Stan had loved being a Marine. He'd been in harm's way on several deployments and yet he'd fallen during a training mission. If he were here, he'd salute those who have served and are serving still. He'd thank his parents and this wonderful community for their support. But he is not here—" Maddie's voice cracked. "So, in his place, I thank you and I accept this award on behalf of Stan and those who made the ultimate sacrifice to protect our freedom."

The applause was deafening. Maddie spotted people wiping tears from their eyes, and even Stan's parents looked moved.

The mayor stood with a good-sized wooden plaque covered in bronze. Stepping up to the mic, he read the engraved words before presenting it to her. "'To our fallen hero, Stan Williams. You are gone, but not forgotten.'"

Maddie trembled as she reached out to accept it. Once that plaque was in her hands, feelings of fraudulence and deceit overwhelmed her. She didn't deserve the heartfelt applause given by the audience. She didn't deserve to stand here like a grieving widow of honor.

The hurt in Stan's eyes after they'd argued that last time flashed before her eyes. After all the times he'd hurt her, she had finally wounded him for real. She'd uttered words she could never take back.

Overcome with nausea, Maddie couldn't return to her seat. Instead, she walked offstage, behind the curtain, and searched for a way out before she got sick. Finding the back-door exit, Maddie opened it, praying an alarm wouldn't sound. She heard nothing but the mayor's final words as she darted outside.

The stinging cold air slapped her hot face, but she

kept running. Maddie ran until she began shivering. She stopped and leaned against a tree, and within seconds she was bent over as one dry heave after another racked her body.

Jackson watched Maddie practically run backstage. Her face had been white as a sheet. He turned to his student conductor and handed him the baton. "Here, Tom. The last song is the national anthem."

"But, Mr. Taylor—"

"You've got this." He'd actually told the boy that he might let him conduct the anthem and to be prepared. It was a great opportunity for him, and he had family in the military. Jackson slapped the boy on the back and then ducked behind the curtain to follow after Maddie.

He looked around, but she wasn't backstage. He heard the mayor invite everyone to stand and sing while the band played the national anthem. That would take a while, so he walked to the back door and opened it.

He spotted Maddie bent over by a tree. She wasn't far away. Thinking she might need a moment to collect herself, Jackson saw her throw down the plaque and kick it. That wasn't grief racking her small frame. That was rage.

He ran toward her, and the closer he got, the louder her sobs. Reaching out, he touched her shoulder and asked the dumbest thing. "Maddie, are you okay?"

"No," she wailed.

He pulled her close and wrapped his arms around her. He wished he could erase her pain, but knew she had to release it first. "It's okay. It's going to be okay."

"No. It's not." She clung to him. "I can't face those people. Not after what I said—I wanted Stan to die."

Those words slapped Jackson hard. "You don't mean that."

Maddie's sobbing had subsided, but she clung to him like a life raft. "It's my fault he's dead. The night before he left for training, we argued. I told him that I hated him and hoped he got killed."

Jackson couldn't believe what he was hearing.

Her fingers bit into his shoulders with a strength he'd not thought possible from someone so delicate. Her voice had grown hoarse. "And he did get killed. Stan's parachute malfunctioned. He ended up dead because of me. Because of what I said. Even in death, it's always been my fault!"

Jackson went cold all over, and it wasn't because of the bitter air. Delia had once told him that she hated him, so he knew how it felt to hear it. But she'd followed up with how she hated what she'd become. She'd said it with such hopeless surrender, Jackson knew it had been the depression talking.

Maddie's words had fire. Livid heat that meant every word. For a split second, Jackson pitied her dead husband. Even Jackson's resentment toward God wasn't as strong as the guilty hatred Maddie spewed. If Jackson's love hadn't been enough to fix Delia, it sure wouldn't fix Maddie, either.

He felt her pull away from him. "I'm sorry to lay this all on you."

"Don't be. Look, Maddie—what can I do?" What could he do?

*Pray.*

He let his hands drop from around her. He really should pray with her, right here and now, but he had to get back before the program ended. They both needed to return.

He watched as she picked up the plaque and held it against her like a shield. Mascara streaked down her cheek, making her look so young and vulnerable that his heart broke.

"There's nothing you can do. I've asked God for forgiveness so many times, but finally admitting it to someone actually helped ease the burden of it, somewhat."

He cringed at the bitterness in her voice. "God has forgiven you, Maddie. You have to forgive you."

Was that enough?

She closed her eyes and more tears leaked out. "How can I?"

He stepped closer and gently wiped away a tear and then the mascara streak. "Have you considered talking to a professional? A licensed counselor or psychologist?"

Her eyes flew open and he could see the hurt there. "No."

"I can give you the name of the family counselor I see with the girls. We go every other month." Jackson should offer to go with her, but he knew this was something she had to work through on her own at first.

"I'll think about it." Maddie still held that plaque in a death grip.

"Come on." He offered his hand, grateful when she took it, but her skin felt so cold. He squeezed. "Let's head back."

They walked across part of the parking lot toward the school. Glancing at her, he could see Maddie still looked hurt and a little lost. Would she really think about seeing a professional? He sure hoped so. She was carrying far too heavy a load.

Still holding Maddie's hand, Jackson opened the back door with a swipe of his school ID. He heard the last notes of the national anthem as they approached the stage. "I don't think we were missed."

"Good." Maddie let go of his hand, but barely looked at him. "I better find my in-laws."

"Okay." He watched her slip through the curtain, gather up her purse and skip down the side steps. He should have prayed with her, but after all he'd said with anger, he didn't know where to start or how to even approach God.

He exited the stage and bounded down the side steps to meet his students in the pit. "Good job, everyone. Thanks, Tom, for stepping in—I knew you could do it, and you were great. The band room is open, if you want to store your instruments. If I don't see you at lunch, then have a good weekend."

"Nice job, son." His dad appeared next to him.

His girls came running toward him next, followed by his mom at a much slower pace. He looked around, but couldn't see where Maddie had gone. "Thanks."

He scooped up Dora. "Hi."

His daughter giggled.

Zoe hugged him. "Good job, Daddy."

"Why, thank you." He bowed, still holding Dora, and heard more giggles.

His mother leaned in to give him a hug. And then she whispered close to his ear, "I saw you embracing your nanny through the ladies' room window. We need to talk."

He knew that tone and sighed.

His mother had always been protective of her family, but after Delia's suicide, she'd become like a bear with her cub. A lecture was no doubt coming. He could kiss goodbye asking his parents to babysit in order to take Maddie out.

He didn't have high hopes of discussing much of anything with Maddie tonight.

* * *

"Are you sure you don't want to come home with me?" Maddie's mom put her car in Park.

"I'm sure. I'm really tired and will probably take a nap." Maddie leaned over and kissed her mother's cheek. "Thank you for driving me home."

"I think you should have kept that plaque."

"Stan's parents appreciated it more." Maddie reached for the door handle. "I'll call you tomorrow."

"Okay, honey. Sleep well."

Maddie waved as her mom backed out and pulled away. She glanced at Jackson's kitchen window and his mother was there.

Sue Taylor looked up, connected with Maddie's gaze and then quickly looked away. Not even a smile.

Maddie shook her head. She'd wanted to make a good impression on Jackson's parents, but had failed somehow. She hoped to get to know them a little better, but it didn't appear that Sue Taylor wanted that. During the luncheon that followed the Veterans Day Program, Sue had been standoffish. And that was too bad.

She unlocked her front door and went inside. What a day! She fell apart in Jackson's arms, had to fake it through a tense lunch with her in-laws, and then there had been her mother's embarrassing remark about how handsome Jackson was when she'd introduced the two.

*Jackson.*

He thought she needed professional help.

"Hellloooo." Pearl rang the bell in her cage. She wanted out.

"Hello, Pearl. How's my pretty bird?"

"Pretty." The parrot fluffed her feathers.

Maddie opened the door of her cage. "Come on. I'll give you a snack."

"Peanuts?"

"Maybe." Maddie was too exhausted to refuse. Too exhausted to rouse any anger at Stan for getting Pearl hooked on them.

The parrot flew down the short hallway and perched on the back of her high chair in the kitchen. Maddie gathered a handful of fresh veggies and chopped them up with a couple of peanuts. She gave some to Pearl and then poured herself a tall glass of water.

Maddie padded in to her small living room, grabbed the blanket off a chair and threw herself onto the couch. She wished she could talk to Jackson, but she didn't want to interrupt his time with his parents. Not to mention, his mother had just snubbed her. She didn't want to make any trouble by forcing her way into their family time.

Maddie snorted. She hadn't let an overprotective mother-in-law prevent her from eloping with Stan. She'd been a different person then. Impulsive and headstrong. Now she was a bitter shell of her old self.

Maybe Sue Taylor had guessed how she felt about her son and stepped in to stand guard over him. Considering everything Jackson had gone through, Maddie could understand the woman's concerns, but it didn't make her feel any better. It didn't make the lack of a smile or acknowledgment any less rude.

Maddie's cell phone dinged with an incoming text. She dragged her purse off the coffee table and pulled out her phone. It was from Jackson.

You okay?

Her heart beat a little faster. If she replied that she wasn't, would he come over? She sure could use his arms around her right about now. That wasn't a good idea, because she might not let him go.

She texted back that she was wiped out but otherwise fine and thanked him for checking.

A few moments later, he replied with the name and number of his family counselor. He also added that if Maddie left a message, the woman would call back within a day or two.

Maddie threw her phone onto the floor and curled into a ball. Remembering how he'd reacted to her confession stung. His embrace had changed once she'd uttered those horrible words about hating her husband. Jackson's arms had slackened around her and his back had straightened up stiff as a board. It was as if he realized he held on to a piece of dynamite that might explode at any minute.

But she didn't explode and she wasn't unstable.

*What if I am?*

Maybe he thought so. If he did, there was no way he'd want anything more than friendship with her. She couldn't really blame him. He'd had a rough marriage too. But Jackson had loved his spouse despite the challenges, and Maddie had grown to hate hers. She didn't deserve a second chance at love.

Maddie lay on the couch completely drained, but sleep wouldn't come. Throwing back the blanket, she made her way into her sewing room. She had stacks of felted wool that needed to be cut into mitten patterns. Grabbing her scissors, she got busy.

It wasn't long before Pearl flew into the room and landed on the perch to preen.

Maddie held up a piece of wool. "What do you think, Pearl? Is this a pretty pattern?"

The parrot whistled. "Pretty."

"I think so too." Despite the heavy feeling in her soul, Maddie chuckled.

Pearl always made her smile and kept her company while she worked. Her whole life, Maddie knew she could depend on one special gray parrot to love her unconditionally. Sure, Maddie's mom loved her, but there had been several men who had pulled her attention away. Pearl was the only constant in her life.

Working with wool was different from her usual fabric choices, but soothing all the same. Maddie had a few ideas to add to her hat-and-mitten line. Scarves, purses, and maybe even coats if she could make the patterns work. She hadn't heard back yet on her loan application, but if she could get the money, she'd buy into that boutique in Marquette. She had to look toward her own future, and she wanted enough inventory to be ready.

She shouldn't count on watching Dora much longer than a couple more months. The little girl started all-day kindergarten next fall, and if the daycare spot became available before Christmas, Jackson might want Dora to go there. That had been the agreement from the beginning.

Maddie didn't want to think that Jackson might not want her to watch his girls after such a meltdown. He'd be honest if that were the case, wouldn't he? She felt the familiar twinge of heartache when she thought about not seeing those girls on a daily basis.

Maybe she did need to talk to someone, but before she called a professional, she might be better served if she finally opened up to Erica and Ruth. Not at church, but at their next lunch. Like her pastor had said, sometimes confession brought forgiveness.

Confessing to Jackson truly had lifted the burden,

but she needed absolution. Erica and Ruth were strong Christian women she trusted. Maddie needed to find out what they thought of her entire situation before she made any big moves.

# *Chapter Twelve*

❧

"Jackson?" his mom called from the bottom of the stairs.

He got up from the recliner in the living room and made his way toward her. "Yeah?"

"The girls want you to say their prayers with them."

Jackson nodded and followed his mother upstairs. His parents had tucked Zoe and Dora into bed and read them a bedtime story. Did Zoe really ask for him to say prayers or was that his mom's idea? Didn't matter. It was his duty as their dad.

Stepping into his girls' room, Jackson knelt between their beds. "Hello, princesses."

They giggled.

"I'm not a princess," Zoe corrected.

"How do you know?"

His oldest shrugged her shoulders.

"I'm a princess." Dora grinned. "Maddie told me so."

Jackson chuckled and tapped Dora's nose. "She's right."

"We'll be downstairs," his mom said. "Good night, girls." His mom and dad gave hugs and kisses to each girl and left, but not before his mom gave him a pointed look.

He wasn't going to get off without having a *talk* with

her. His mom had waited until the girls were tucked safely in bed. Even if he'd wanted to ask Maddie out for tonight, she was too emotionally drained. Understandably too. She didn't need him adding to her stress by asking if they might date. That could wait.

Zoe reached out to him. "Hold my hand."

He took both Zoe's and Dora's hands, stretching his arms between their beds. He bowed his head. "Go ahead, Zoe."

"Will you pray this time, Daddy?"

His heart pinched. "Okay. You fill in what I miss."

Zoe nodded and closed her eyes. Dora did too.

"Dear Lord," Jackson started.

No sooner had he said it than his throat tightened with emotion. He closed his eyes with humility. After all his anger and insults, Jackson wasn't worthy to approach the Throne of God. No one was and that was the whole point. God loved him anyway. He'd always been one prayer away.

*Dear Lord, I'm sorry.*

He'd failed in so many ways. He cleared his throat. "God bless Grandma and Grandpa and Aunt Mel and be with Maddie tonight."

He prayed she was truly okay.

"And take care of Mommy," Zoe whispered.

Jackson felt his throat swelling up again and his eyes stung. Would the Lord still care for his wife after her overdose? What conversations might she have had with God before she passed? For all he knew, Delia might finally be free, her healing complete. Like Maddie had said, maybe God didn't get the chance to heal her on earth. He fervently prayed so. "And take care of Mommy. Amen."

"Amen," his daughters chorused.

Jackson squeezed their hands, then kissed each girl's forehead before leaving the door open only an inch. A new round night-light sprayed tiny stars across their ceiling. Another gift from Grandma and Grandpa. A good one too. The girls loved it.

He stepped into his bedroom to get control of his emotions before going downstairs. He uttered a silent prayer for guidance. He wanted to trust God again, but he wasn't sure how.

*Lord, I've been a fool. Please forgive me.*

It was a start.

Jackson descended the stairs and found his mom in the kitchen, putting the teakettle on to boil. Her remedy for tough conversations. He didn't beat around the bush. "Okay, what's on your mind?"

His mother looked up over her reading glasses. "Isn't it a little soon to get involved?"

"Maybe."

His mother sighed. "Jackson, this Maddie might be a wonderful girl, but you've only just met her."

*Only fools rush in.*

"I know." He'd had those same thoughts, but his heart didn't listen to his brain very well. It never had.

"What about the girls?"

"They love her." His girls would need a constant feminine influence as they grew older, and Maddie already had their stamp of approval. No problem there.

"All the more reason to be careful. What if you two broke up?"

"We haven't even gone out." Jackson wasn't playing the field; he wanted to see if he and Maddie could make something permanent. They'd have to date to do that. Sure, they could break up, but knowing her thus far, he thought that unlikely.

His mother shook her head. "It's only been a year since Delia's death. You've only just started to heal."

So she thought. His mother had his father. "Look, Mom, I'm tired of raising the girls alone. I'm tired of being alone. Delia may have died twelve months ago, but I was pretty much on my own well before that."

His mom's eyes softened. "I'm so sorry, honey. I just don't want to see you make another mistake."

He narrowed his gaze. This was the first time his mom had admitted that his marriage had been a mistake. He'd loved his wife and he wouldn't trade their two little girls for anything, but knowing what he knew now, would he have made the same decision? He wasn't sure. Not really.

"She seems very emotional." His mother stared him down, challenging him to correct her first impression.

He couldn't, but his mother didn't know the whole story. She didn't know the abuse Maddie had been subjected to, or how accepting that award had affected her. "It was an emotional day for her."

The teakettle whistle blew, but his mother didn't look away. Ignoring the sound, she cupped his face instead. "I just want you to be careful."

He covered her hand. "I want to be careful too. Now, make your tea."

His mother gave his shoulder a pat before finally turning off the gas burner and silencing the whistle. "Do you want a cup?"

"Sure." Jackson wasn't much of a hot tea drinker, but he welcomed anything that might settle the turmoil going on inside him.

As much as he didn't want to agree, his mother was right. He needed to use caution when approaching a romantic relationship with Maddie. Especially now, after hearing about the guilt she carried for hating her husband. She still had things to work through. He did too. Could they do it together?

*God, help me know what to do.*

While his mom fixed two cups of chamomile tea, Jackson searched for a sense of how he should proceed. God wasn't answering him. But then, Jackson had always been an impatient believer—wanting answers now rather than later.

The only thing that kept coming to his mind were the words he'd spoken to Zoe about Maddie's parrot. *Only fools rush in.* And Jackson had been a fool about a lot of things.

Monday, Maddie received another text from Jackson. This one simply stated that Zoe was going home after school with the daughter of one of his fellow middle-school teachers. It would be just the three of them for dinner, if Maddie wished to stay and eat with him and Dora.

She'd texted back that she would make chili and corn bread. It was what she'd planned on making at home anyway. Jackson had extra fixings, so she'd make more than enough for the three of them.

All afternoon, she'd tried to read between the lines of that text and couldn't. Maddie had been happy to see Jackson at church Sunday morning. He appeared to have attended willingly, but his parents had come too. Maddie didn't linger long after the service and had spoken to Jackson and his girls and his parents only briefly.

She should have called Jackson after his parents left late Sunday evening, but Maddie had chickened out, deciding that if he'd wanted to see her, he could have come to her. When he didn't, she'd agonized over whether the kiss they shared had meant little to him, or the confession she'd made about Stan had meant too much. Both were troublesome, and so Maddie had lain low.

Maddie pulled the corn bread out of the oven and set it on the stove to cool. It smelled like home. Her mother made the best corn bread and Maddie had used her recipe. She hoped Jackson liked it. The Heath women made their corn bread a little heavier and sweeter than most. She turned off the oven and set the pot holders aside.

Dora yanked on Maddie's sweater. "Wanna play hide-and-seek?"

The chili was pretty much done and would remain hot in the Crock-Pot. Checking the clock on the wall, she saw Jackson wouldn't be home for an hour yet. Maddie slapped her hands against her knees as she bent down. "Sure, but here's the rules—we have to hide somewhere downstairs. No upstairs. I'll hide first and you come find me."

"Okay." Dora grinned.

Maddie looked around and then pointed toward the wall on the other side of the kitchen table. "If you will count to ten over there and keep your eyes closed, I'll go hide."

Dora nodded, ran over to the corner and shielded her eyes with chubby little hands. "One, two, fwee, four, five…"

Maddie ran for the living room, choosing to duck behind the recliner. She pulled a knitted afghan over herself.

"Ready or not, here I come," Dora yelled out.

Maddie crouched down lower. She heard Dora's giggles as she looked in the laundry closet before coming into the living room.

It didn't take long.

Dora poked the afghan and laughed. "Got you!"

Maddie wrapped the throw around Dora and scooped

up the giggling child. "You sure did. Now it's your turn to hide."

"Go in the kitchen and count." Dora pointed.

Maddie narrowed her gaze. "You already have your hiding place figured out, don't you?"

Dora shrugged, but her lips quivered. It must be a doozy of a place.

"Okay, here I go." Maddie walked back into the kitchen and hid her face against the wall. She slowly counted to ten. Turning, she called out, "Here I come."

Maddie checked under the kitchen table first. Nothing. Then she looked under the dining room table before searching the side porch entry. Still nothing. Smiling, Maddie headed for the living room.

She searched behind the couch. Then she headed for the main entrance and opened the closet door in the foyer. Shuffling through coats, she didn't find a four-year-old huddling beneath them. Closing the door, Maddie spun around.

*Where on earth did Dora go?*

She double-checked the laundry area. Could she squeeze in between the dryer and the side shelves? Nope. Maddie retraced her steps back into the kitchen and opened the pantry door. No Dora. She'd pretty much covered the downstairs. The rooms were large, but Jackson didn't have a ton of furniture filling them.

Maddie checked the porch off the kitchen that overlooked the backyard. It was mid-November and still no snow, but it was much too cold for a little girl to huddle outside. Unless she still had the knitted throw, then maybe. Maddie dashed through the kitchen and dining room to the side door. Still no Dora. Alarmed now, Maddie checked the side porch.

Then the garage. "Dora? Where are you, honey?"

No answer.

It dawned on her that Dora might have gone upstairs even though she wasn't supposed to. Maddie did not want to search those rooms. Especially Jackson's, but she didn't have a choice. Reentering the house through the side door, Maddie climbed the stairs. She opened the first door that appeared to be a guest bedroom and stepped in. "Dora?"

Still no answer.

Maddie looked under the bed and in the closet. Still no child. Her irritation rose. If she found Jackson's daughter somewhere up here after she specifically told her not to hide upstairs, there'd be trouble. Time-out might be involved, and Jackson would definitely be told as well.

Maddie thoroughly checked the girls' room and closet, then the full bathroom, but came up empty-handed. That left Jackson's room. Maddie cringed as she entered, feeling like a trespasser. She looked for places where Dora might hide rather than snooping around.

She scanned the large room with a large bed, chair and a nightstand. A couple of dressers stood against the bare walls. Large frames of either pictures or artwork were leaned against the wall as well, but they were backing-side faced out with no room for a small child to shimmy in between.

Maddie peeked under the bed. There was nothing, not even a lone sock, under there. She checked the walk-in closet and tried to ignore the faint scent of Jackson's cologne that hung in the air. He kept his space tidy.

Next came the remodeled master bathroom, but there were no places to hide, as the tub and huge shower were all open, no shower curtains needed. Even the towels were neatly folded where they hung. She opened the door of the toiletry closet, but it was much too thin for a small child to climb into and Dora wasn't there.

"Lord, please help me find her." Maddie spotted the clock on Jackson's nightstand. She'd been searching for almost half an hour.

She exited to the hallway and checked the ceiling for a draw-down door to the attic, but decided against searching up there since the handle was too high for her to reach, much less a four-year-old.

Frantic, Maddie went back downstairs and yelled, "Dora!"

Surely, Dora hadn't gone to her house, but then, maybe when Maddie hadn't found her, she'd decided to go see Pearl or look for her. Maddie dashed out the side door without bothering to grab her coat. She ran across the two driveways and opened her front door. "Dora?"

"Maddieeeee?" Pearl, locked in her cage like Maddie had left her, flapped her wings.

"Oh, Pearl, did you see Dora come in here?" Knowing the parrot wouldn't be able to answer that question, Maddie ran through her small house, checking each room and calling out Dora's name. Still nothing.

She was on the verge of freaking out. Had someone taken her? Maddie's mind went to wild places and icy fingers of fear nearly choked her. Pulling her phone out of her pocket, Maddie called Jackson first.

"Hey, Maddie—"

She cut him off. "Jackson, I can't find Dora anywhere."

"I'll be right there."

Maddie pocketed her phone and looked up at the ceiling. "Please, God, let her be okay."

Then she ran back next door and searched the basement. It was a vast open space with fluorescent lighting and cream-colored walls and floor. Scanning the laundry hookups and utility sink, she could see there were few places a child could hide down here. There were no outside doors, nooks or crannies.

Quickly, Maddie looked through a few empty cardboard boxes that hadn't yet been broken down. Nothing. Dora wasn't there. She was gone.

Jackson dashed into his house. His heart hadn't stopped racing ever since Maddie had called. He'd prayed the whole way home. Hard. Begging God for mercy.

"Dora! Dora, where are you?"

Maddie met him at the side entrance. She looked awful and very afraid. "I've searched everywhere."

He ran a hand through his hair. "What were you doing?"

"We were playing hide-and-seek. It was her turn to hide. The rules were simple—stay downstairs." She slapped her hand over her mouth and fresh tears filled her eyes.

He couldn't believe Dora would step outside, but then, she was only four. "Okay, where have you looked?"

"Everywhere. Upstairs, the basement, the porches, the garage—my house."

Jackson checked his watch, trying to stay calm. "How long has it been?"

"I don't know. An hour?"

"I'm going to check upstairs." He lunged up the stairs, taking them two at a time, with Maddie stomping her way up behind him.

Calling out his daughter's name again and again, he opened every door, asking Maddie if she'd looked in each space.

"Yes, yes, I looked everywhere." Tears ran freely down Maddie's cheeks.

Jackson didn't like this at all. If Dora was in trouble, he was wasting time retracing where Maddie had been. He jogged back down the steps.

Maddie followed.

He tore open the front entry closet door and slammed back the coats hanging there. No Dora!

"One more time, where might you not have looked, think of anywhere you might have missed?" He stepped toward her and his voice rose.

Maddie took a step back, her eyes wide.

Seeing the fear he felt reflected in her eyes, Jackson lost it. He reached out and gripped her upper arms. "How could you lose my daughter!"

Maddie's face paled. Even her blue eyes went nearly gray with terror as she pulled away from him. "I'm sorry!"

He'd crossed the line. He never should have put his hands on her. Not like that. But he didn't have time to apologize right now. He pulled out his phone, feeling like his world was caving in. "I have to call 911."

Maddie had backed up against the wall under the stairs.

Jackson looked for the little block of wood that he'd tapped into place with a lousy finishing nail at the top of the secret door. It had come loose and fallen off.

He'd never gotten around to permanently sealing the entrance to the secret room under the stairs. He didn't think Maddie knew about that hidden alcove. If she had, she would have said something. It was no wonder she couldn't find Dora.

He felt sick. What if—

He heard a sleepy-sounding cry and tapped the door. It opened and there stood his daughter, rubbing her eyes, a knitted throw barely clinging to her shoulders.

His knees nearly gave out with relief before anger washed through him: "Dora, how could you hide in there? You scared the daylights out of us!"

He picked Dora up, holding her close when she started to cry in earnest, and glanced at Maddie. She had slid down to the floor and was holding her head in her hands. "Maddie, I'm so sorry."

She got to her feet but looked a little unsteady. Her face had regained some of its normal color but was blotchy. She didn't look scared anymore, but haunted, as if she'd been through this too many times before.

When she finally faced him, her expression was oddly bland. "I can't do this."

"Maddie, listen—"

She placed her finger to his lips to shush him. And then she reached out and rubbed his daughter's back. "I have to go."

Dora was still crying and Jackson tried to comfort her while helplessly watching Maddie grab her coat and walk out the door. It felt terrifying, like she was walking out of his life.

"Dora, it's okay. You can stop crying now." He couldn't leave things with Maddie like this.

"You're mad." Dora hiccuped, but she was calming down.

"I was, but now I'm not." He was more furious with himself for not fixing that door properly and for not thinking to give Maddie a heads-up about it.

"Come on. Let's get you into a coat and boots. We have to go tell Maddie we're sorry." He'd never taken off his jacket.

"Why?" Dora sniffed.

Jackson grabbed a tissue. "Here, blow."

Dora did so with her usual giggle. No harm done.

"Because we both scared Maddie."

Dora pursed her lips together. The sweet face of innocent contrition. His baby hadn't meant to do something so wrong.

He would have laughed had his heart not been so heavy. How long would it take to erase the fear he'd seen in Maddie's eyes? Fear of him!

After bundling up his daughter in a coat and hat and mittens and boots, he carried her across his driveway and Maddie's. When he reached Maddie's house, he knocked on the front door.

When she didn't answer, he knocked again. "Maddie? I know you know I'm out here. Dora's with me and we want to apologize for scaring you."

He looked at Dora and smiled. He could hear Pearl squawking in the background.

"Maddie?"

After a few seconds, she finally answered through the door, without opening it. "There's nothing to talk about."

"Yes, there is. Please forgive me for losing control. I was scared too." If he ever truly lost one of his kids, it might be the end of him. Surely, she could understand where he was coming from. His outburst was about fear, not anger.

Silence.

"Maddie?"

"This is my issue. I can't deal with anger directed at me. Even if it's justified. I'm sorry, but I can't do this anymore. I can't be what you want."

"You *are* what I want." There, he'd finally said it out loud.

"Jackson, please, go."

He glanced at his daughter.

Dora looked back as if trying to make sense of this whole conversation. "Can we see Pearl?"

Jackson shook his head. "Not today."

"Why?"

"Because Maddie's not feeling well after such a big scare. Come on. Let's go home."

"Okay."

Jackson trekked back over their driveways and into his house when his phone dinged with an incoming text. He put Dora down and checked his screen. His hopes lifted when he saw the message was from Maddie.

I will continue to watch the girls until you either find someone else or the daycare spot opens up.

He texted back his thanks.

At least Maddie wasn't bailing on Dora and Zoe, just him. Still, he'd check with the daycare and see where he stood on their waiting list. He'd give Maddie space for now, but eventually they'd have to talk about this. She was the woman he wanted. He wasn't going to let her issues from a previous marriage, nor his, stand in their way.

Fools might rush in, but they also rushed out. And Jackson was done being a fool. He was in this for the long haul. With God's help, no matter how much time it took, he'd prove to Maddie that she could trust him.

# Chapter Thirteen

It had been several days since Maddie couldn't find Dora. She made sure to leave as soon as Jackson came home on Tuesday, Wednesday and Thursday. She hadn't stayed for dinner, even though he'd asked her to. Even though the girls had asked as well.

Was she horrible for ducking out on Jackson when she knew he wanted to talk about what had happened? Probably.

Over and over she'd played what he'd said in her mind. Jackson hadn't done anything wrong. Not really. He hadn't physically harmed her nor had he insulted her, but he'd scared her. Her reaction might be understandable, considering her married life with Stan, but it went much deeper.

If Maddie were to follow her heart into a relationship with Jackson, would she shrink into an emotional ball every time they argued? If he ever raised his voice, would she simply give in to keep the peace? She'd had her fill of all that with Stan. This was her issue, one she wasn't sure how to fix. She also didn't want to put Zoe and Dora through any more emotional upheaval. They'd been through enough with their mom.

Add to that the fact that this morning, Maddie had

been turned down for the loan she'd requested with a call from her bank, and she really needed to unload. The only two people who'd not only understand but give her straight-up wisdom were Ruth and Erica. It was time to come clean because she needed their advice.

After getting out of her car, Maddie took a deep breath and walked into the Pine Inn Café. Ruth and Erica were already seated at their regular table, saw her and waved.

Maddie slipped into a seat. "Hi."

Erica touched her shoulder. "Are you okay? You look upset."

"No. I'm not. Okay, that is." Maddie started to cry, then gave a wobbly-sounding laugh as she took her glasses off and wiped her face with a napkin. "I'm sorry."

Ruth gripped her hand. "What's going on?"

"I don't even know where to start." Maddie took a sip of her water and tried to get control of her emotions.

Ruth and Erica exchanged a look.

"How about at the beginning," Erica said.

"My dad left when I was seven—" Maddie paused for effect.

Both Ruth and Erica looked worried.

Maddie gave a sad chuckle. "I'm joking. I won't go back that far. The truth is that I never should have married Stan. I was young and stupid when we eloped. I never realized how emotionally abusive he was until after I inherited Pearl. Maybe he was jealous of the connection I had with her, or resented the care I gave her."

Maddie stopped when the waitress came to take their orders. She didn't feel much like eating, but since she hadn't had breakfast, she needed something and asked for a grilled chicken sandwich.

"Go on," Ruth said once the waitress left.

She didn't want to ramble, but needed to set the stage

for what had happened with Jackson. She wanted to know if she was overreacting, or if she'd made the right decision to break it off. "I left Stan once, but he found me, stole Pearl and threatened to kill her if I didn't return. So, I stayed. The night before he was killed we argued, and I told him that I hoped he didn't make it home."

Erica's eyes widened. "So, that's why you feel guilty."

Maddie nodded. "He was the only one in a parachute jump that died because of a chute malfunction. How do I know he didn't do it on purpose because of what I'd said?"

"Oh, Maddie." Erica reached out and grabbed her hand. "Even if that were true, which I doubt, the decision was on him. His choice."

Maddie nodded, thinking of what Jackson had told her about forgiving herself. "It's hard, though. I never should have said what I did."

"All of us have said things we shouldn't have in the heat of an argument," Ruth said.

"Yeah, but I meant every word." Maddie leaned back as the waitress delivered their meals. "There's more, though. Monday, I couldn't find Dora. We played hide-and-seek, and she hid in this secret room under their stairs that I didn't know about. Her dad had sealed it off, but not very well. Anyway, when we couldn't find her, he flipped out."

"What did he do?" Ruth took a bite of her salad.

"He gripped my arms and yelled at me. He didn't hurt me physically, but I felt thrown back into my marriage." Remembering the intensity in Jackson's voice, the frantic outrage, made her shudder.

"What did he say when he yelled?" Erica asked.

"How could I lose his daughter." Maddie would never forget the accusation in his voice.

"He didn't call you names or anything, did he?"

Maddie shook her head. "No."

"You care for him but you're scared," Erica said.

"Very scared. I don't want to make another mistake."

"Do you love him?" Ruth asked.

"I'm not sure I know what real love is." Maddie spread her hands, but moved on. She was on a roll and it actually felt good, as if she'd unloaded something too heavy to keep carrying. "Remember me telling you about that boutique in Marquette?"

Ruth and Erica both nodded.

"Well, the loan I applied for got turned down because they'll only lend up to eighty-five percent of the value. If I sold my house outright, I'd get back the money I put down, which is what I need to buy into that store."

"But you'd be moving away from Jackson and his girls," Ruth said.

"I love those girls, and I don't want to see them hurt. If I get out now, they'll move on, but if I stay and it still doesn't work out with Jackson, then what?" She'd be even worse off than she was now. They all would.

"Oh, Maddie, I'm sorry." Ruth grabbed her hand and squeezed. "That's a tough place to be, but you have to take care of you first."

"I don't know how to do that." Maddie wanted to sell her house and run, but was that the right thing to do or was it just the safest? It felt like she'd been running away from conflict her whole life. She wished she had the gumption to stay and fight.

"Is there no other way to get the money?" Erica asked.

Maddie shook her head. "I don't think my mother has that kind of cash. Even if she did, I wouldn't feel right asking. If her new husband said no, that would always be between us."

Erica was looking at her closely, her cheeseburger temporarily forgotten. "What is it that you really want?"

"I've wanted to sell my designs forever." Maddie didn't want to lose this opportunity. It was her first real chance to do things on her own terms.

"And Jackson?"

"I just don't think I can handle a romantic relationship." Again, Maddie heard Jackson's words about seeing a professional. Maybe he was right. Maybe she needed help with her past before she could even think about her future, one that included him.

"I think we should pray right here, right now, that God will intervene in Maddie's situation. Perfect love casts out fear, and God provides what we need if we ask Him." Erica offered a hand to each of them.

Ruth smiled and reached out her hands as well.

Maddie hesitated only a moment before latching on to Erica and Ruth. She didn't deserve God's provisions. "Someone else has to pray, though."

"Of course." Erica led them in a quick but powerful prayer. She asked God to bless all of them with second chances, and for Maddie specifically, Erica prayed for clarity and healing and forgiveness.

"Amen." Maddie wanted all those things, but would God see fit to grant them? Only time would tell.

Late Friday afternoon, Jackson hoped the two half-gallon containers of ice cream he'd purchased might persuade Maddie to finally talk to him. He'd given her space this whole week, watching her leave as soon as he got home without complaint. Okay, so maybe it had only been four days, but it felt like forever to him.

It wasn't as if he'd ever pressure her to stay, but she'd turned down his dinner invitation yesterday. She'd made pot roast for him and the girls, but she wouldn't stay to enjoy it with them, and that hurt. With the Christmas concert less than three weeks away, band practice and rehearsals were ramping up. He'd have to stay after school a few more days than normal to catch up since they'd lose all of next week's after-school rehearsals due to the Thanksgiving holiday.

"Can we eat the ice cream right away?" Zoe asked.

"I don't see why not." Seemed like he was making a habit of dessert before dinner on Fridays. A good start to the weekend for sure. Pulling into his driveway, he cut the engine and grabbed the grocery bag of ice cream.

Zoe slipped out of her booster seat in the back and pointed. "There's a paper on the door."

He walked up the side porch steps and grabbed a note from Maddie that Dora was at her house. It'd be harder to talk to her there with the girls in such close proximity. Maybe she'd planned for that. "Come on. Let's see if we can eat our ice cream over at Maddie's house."

Zoe darted for the front door and opened it.

"Zoe, wait. We should knock first."

"Maddie won't mind. Come on." His daughter motioned for him to hurry, and then she walked right in.

"Hello?" Jackson knocked on the door before entering. His eldest daughter was already inside, out of her coat, hat and mittens.

"We're in the sewing room."

He followed Zoe down the short hallway to the second bedroom that Maddie used to make her designs. Standing in the doorway, he spotted Dora sitting on the floor with child scissors, cutting a piece of what looked like tissue paper. Maddie sewed together something larger than mittens, the rhythmic sound of the sewing machine drowning out everything else.

Zoe approached the parrot. "Hello, Pearl."

"Hellloooo," Pearl cooed.

Jackson smiled. His girls loved that parrot.

"Daddy!" Dora jumped up and ran to hug his knees.

He scooped her up. "Hello, Miss Dora."

Maddie pushed her glasses up the bridge of her nose as she looked at him. "Sorry, I sort of lost track of time."

"No worries. I read the note."

"But I saw it first," Zoe clarified.

"You sure did, Zoe. I brought ice cream, if you'd like to take a break." He thought he saw Maddie's eyes light up a little when he lifted the brown paper bag.

"Sure. Why don't we go into the kitchen?" Maddie stood. "Zoe, if you'd like to bring Pearl, hold out your hand for her."

"Come on, Pearl." Zoe smiled when the parrot walked onto her arm from the perch.

Jackson smiled. "She really is a pretty bird."

"Pretty bird," Pearl mimicked.

To think the parrot had given him the creeps at first. He'd never realized how affectionate a bird could be. Or how much of a personality they might have.

He still carried Dora as he followed behind Maddie and Zoe. Once in the kitchen, he set her down. His youngest joined Zoe at Pearl's high chair. The parrot perched on the back and fluttered her feathers.

"Peanuts?" Pearl asked.

"No, Pearl. No peanuts," Maddie answered.

Jackson set the bag on the counter and pulled out two cartons. "I brought vanilla and mint chocolate chip."

Maddie came to stand next to him. She opened the drawer and grabbed four spoons. "Sounds good to me."

He reached for her wrist, stilling her. "What's your favorite flavor?"

Her gaze flew to his, more surprised than fearful, and then she pulled away. "Anything with chocolate."

He watched her as she grabbed four bowls from the cupboard and lined them up on the counter. He hated that she kept her distance from him. Hated that he still scared her. He never should have lost it that way, never should have yelled at her, but he'd been afraid too. Scared of losing his daughter. Even so, that look of terror on Maddie's face when he'd gripped her arms ate at him still.

Maddie retrieved an ice-cream scoop from another drawer. Keeping her head down, she asked, "What would the girls like?"

"Zoe will take a little of each. Vanilla for Dora, and both for me."

She nodded.

He stepped closer and kept his voice low. "Maddie, can't we talk?"

As she scooped ice cream into the bowls, she never looked up. "There's nothing to talk about. This is my issue."

He glanced at his girls, who were busy with Pearl, so he took a chance. "Even though I yelled, I'd never hurt you. I'd never raise my hand to you."

Surely, she didn't think he would.

She finally faced him. "But I'll go into victim mode every time you do yell. Don't you see? I can't put you through that. Or the girls. I won't."

His heart broke. Maybe in time, if she'd get some help. "Have you called the counselor I meet with? She might shed some light on what you're going through."

She shook her head. "Not yet."

"Call her, Maddie."

She scooped the last serving of ice cream and set the

bowls on the kitchen table, effectively shutting down the conversation. Evidently, it was her way or the highway.

He had to admit that Maddie had an inner strength that Delia had lacked, but at least Delia had never feared him. Regardless, both women battled inner dragons he couldn't slay.

*God, what should I do?*

Jackson clenched and then unclenched his hands before sitting down at the table to eat ice cream he no longer wanted.

He couldn't push her. He couldn't beg or plead his case. He needed to pray for Maddie because it was really all he could do. Still, his heart sank. He'd been here before. Too many times, in fact.

Would God answer this time, before all was lost? He sure hoped so.

Maddie leaned against the door once Jackson and his girls left. She believed he finally understood why she couldn't pursue a relationship with him. It was torture watching his face fall with those sad blue eyes when it appeared to have finally clicked. She'd had to grit her teeth to keep from backtracking. It had taken everything she had to ignore that tug on her heart to change her mind.

*It's better this way. Better to cut the strings now.*

*It doesn't feel better.*

Not wanting to dwell on it, Maddie got busy cleaning her house. She had an appointment with a Realtor later this evening. If she could sell for at least the price she'd paid, she'd do it. Ruth and Erica had been right. It was time to pursue her dream and take care of herself for a while.

After vacuuming and dusting, Maddie grabbed the basket where she stored her mail. She kept it on a little table near the front door. As she pulled out the envelopes, a small piece of paper fluttered to the floor.

Maddie picked it up. The name and phone number of Jackson's family counselor were written on it. Had he stuck the paper in with her mail before he'd left? Irritation seared through her, but then it turned into an odd appreciation. Jackson cared. He really did.

Could she work through the mess of her past by simply talking about it? She'd sort of already done that and it had helped her feel lighter, but nothing had changed. She was still the same girl who was afraid of making another mistake. The same girl who couldn't handle confrontation.

Maddie searched for her cell phone and punched the number she'd saved in her contacts. Talking to a professional counselor might be worth a try. She had nothing to lose at this point. As she walked to the kitchen, she waited for voice mail to kick in after the rings.

"Hello, this is Dr. Savannah."

Maddie hadn't expected to talk to her, especially on a Friday night. "Ummm, hello. Hi, my name is Maddie Williams. Jackson Taylor gave me your name and number."

"Hi, Maddie, what can I do for you?"

Maddie took a deep breath and let it back out. "I'm tired of living in fear. Can you help me?"

The woman chuckled. "A lot depends on you. How willing are you to accept God's promises?"

Maddie's heart leaped. Jackson hadn't mentioned that he met with a Christian counselor. A believer like her. "But what if I don't deserve those promises?"

"None of us do, but God is faithful to restore us if we're willing to let go of what binds us. Would you like to meet?"

Maddie's hand trembled. "Yes. Yes, I would."

"I had a cancellation first thing Tuesday morning, if that works for you."

"It does." Maddie grabbed a pen and jotted down the exact time and location before wrapping up the call.

Maddie pocketed her cell phone and stood in the middle of her kitchen, overwhelmed by a sense of awe. God had not only heard Erica's prayer, but He'd hand-delivered this appointment.

*God answers prayer.*

Maddie vowed to do her part. This felt like a step in the right direction and she didn't want to mess it up. She'd have to drive all the way to Jackson's hometown of Escanaba, but she'd make it back to Pine in time to pick up Dora from preschool. And then she'd say goodbye for a few days while Jackson took his girls to his parents' house for Thanksgiving.

She missed them already. What would it be like when she no longer lived next door? The doorbell rang, scattering her thoughts.

Maddie opened her door and welcomed the same Realtor who'd listed the house when Maddie bought it. "Hi. Come on in."

After some short pleasantries, the agent got down to business. "You're selling pretty quickly after moving in, but the good news is there's a shortage of homes in this price range. You should do pretty well."

"I hope so. Let me show you the changes I've made since buying." Maddie had painted all the rooms a warm ivory and installed new carpet throughout the living room and bedrooms.

After the short tour, Maddie offered her Realtor coffee as they went over paperwork and possible listing prices. Maddie went over with the agent what she needed to clear in order to buy into the boutique in Marquette. She didn't have the wiggle room to discount for a quick sale. She needed to sell at the high end of the price range for a home her size in order to recoup her original down payment. It'd be tight and might be a long shot, but Maddie decided to trust that God would answer one way or another. If the house sold quickly, Maddie was on her way to Marquette. If it didn't, then she'd have to find another way to sell her wool designs.

Without hesitation, Maddie signed on the dotted line. The Realtor explained the timeline before her house went live online and a for-sale sign was placed in her front yard. Both would happen the following week.

Maddie nodded, hoping it would be after Jackson left for Escanaba. She didn't relish telling him she was moving. The defeat in his eyes earlier this afternoon had been bad enough.

It was late by the time her agent left. Maddie made her way back to the kitchen to clear the coffee mugs and give Pearl a before-bedtime snack. As she stood at the sink, Maddie's gaze was automatically drawn across their two driveways to Jackson's kitchen window.

He stood at his sink, and it looked like he was rinsing dinner dishes before loading them in the dishwasher.

Watching him made her heart ache. She wished things were different. She wished she was different. Maddie prayed for her upcoming appointment, and then she prayed for Jackson. She hoped he'd find the right woman to make a new life with. Him and the girls. It hurt to say that prayer, but Maddie couldn't be what he needed. She was too damaged.

Just then, Jackson looked up and held her gaze. He looked tired. And sad.

Maddie raised her hand to wave, but she barely wiggled her fingers.

He repeated the gesture back to her and mouthed the words *sleep tight*.

"You too." Her eyes teared up. She'd never felt so help-lessly heartbroken.

## Chapter Fourteen

Jackson pulled into his driveway with Zoe buckled up in her booster seat. He didn't bother going into the garage, even though snow fell softly from the sky. They'd be leaving for his parents' house soon.

The season's first snow came late and there was more on the way. He wanted to get on the road before it turned heavy. He shut off the engine and got out. A line of snow had already accumulated along the edge of the driveway where it met grass. With the ground nearly frozen from the cold temperatures they'd had, the snow would stick. And then it would pile up.

Zoe clamored out of her seat and shut the door. She stood with her mouth open, trying to catch a few flakes.

Jackson laughed. "Come on, Zoe. We've got to load up and head for Grandma and Grandpa's so we make it by dinnertime."

Zoe caught one more snowflake, then dashed inside, zipping in front of him.

Jackson wondered how Maddie might be today. Yesterday, she'd seemed keyed up and tense. He stepped over Zoe's coat on the floor where she'd left it. "Zoe, hang up your coat, would you?"

"But I'm just going to put it back on again." She slipped it onto a hook on the hall tree.

"That's why we have these hooks, silly girl."

Zoe giggled and darted off toward the kitchen.

"Daddy!" Dora came running for him, her arms wide open.

He scooped her up and kissed her cheek. "How's my princess today?"

"Good."

"Ready to go see Grandma and Grandpa?" He carried her through the dining room, bouncing her in his arms the whole way.

Dora shrugged.

"What?"

"Can't we stay wif Maddie and Pearl?"

Jackson had entered the kitchen just as Dora spoke. He'd love to share Thanksgiving with Maddie and even her parrot, but she'd made her feelings clear. He glanced at Maddie to see if she'd heard Dora.

"Sorry, Dora, but I have to go to my mom's house. And you need to see your grandparents." Maddie had heard.

He set Dora on her feet and then he asked, "How are you?"

Maddie gave him a tight smile laced with regret. "Working through some things."

"Welcome to the club." He chuckled, but it sounded hollow. No amusement there. "I've got to load the car. Would you mind giving the girls a snack?"

"No problem. I made peanut butter cookies for your trip."

He spotted the plastic container and grinned. "Can I have one now?"

"Of course. I'll get some cheese and crackers for the girls." Maddie turned to open the fridge.

He opened the container and grabbed two cookies but never took his eyes off Maddie as she pulled out a block of cheddar and headed for the counter. She seemed relaxed, and she'd made cookies. A sign of good things ahead?

Probably too early to tell.

He took a bite. "Oh, wow. These are great."

She smiled. "Thanks."

"I want a cookie." Dora climbed into a seat at the table.

"Of course you do." Jackson's youngest had taken after him when it came to baked goods. Zoe was more of an ice-cream hound.

Maddie placed a cookie on a paper plate for each girl next to stacks of crackers and cheese and apple slices. Then she waved him away. "Go pack. I've got this."

Of course she did. Jackson fetched his oldest from the living room, where she watched TV. "Zoe, Maddie has your snack ready in the kitchen. I'm going to load the car."

"Okay." She hopped off the couch and ran for the kitchen.

Jackson turned off the TV with a click, grateful that neither of his girls had any idea of the tension between him and Maddie. He needed to let things settle before approaching her again. He hoped she'd called Dr. Savannah, but he couldn't keep pushing her. It was her decision to make.

He prayed for Maddie instead. Daily. He prayed for his daughters too and was amazed at the peace God had given him. Peace he didn't deserve, but he'd accept with gratitude. Trust was a choice, and he was choosing to trust God from here on out. He had to. The alternative didn't lead anywhere healthy.

He ran up the stairs and gathered up the two small

suitcases he'd packed last night. One for him, and one for his girls. He also grabbed their activity bag stuffed with coloring books and dolls. Zoe's mama elephant slipped out onto the floor.

He set everything down in order to grab it. As he picked it up, he noticed a scrap of paper tucked into the stuffed animal's dress pocket. He pulled out a folded photograph. As he opened it, his breath caught at the picture of his late wife as a teenager looking out from the glossy paper with a wide smile. Delia must have given it to Zoe, because Jackson had never seen this photo before.

He flipped it over and read what Delia had written on the back—*I love you, Zoe. Now and always.*

He went down on his knees and closed his eyes to keep the tears at bay. Why'd she rob their little girls of their mother? It wasn't fair to any of them.

He tucked the photo back in place. He knew memories were not enough. His girls needed more than just written words of love. He needed more too.

Jackson zeroed in on his wedding ring. A simple band of gold. That wasn't enough, either. Delia might have loved them, but she'd left them. He slipped off the band and walked back to his bedroom closet, dropping it into the box of keepsakes meant for his girls when they got older. Delia's wedding set and jewels were in there, as well as her diaries, written when she was a young girl.

He ran his fingers across the box, wondering when the indentation of his wedding band might fade from his skin. He wasn't married anymore. He was widowed. The anger was gone, leaving behind a sad acceptance of losing his wife well before she died.

He couldn't help but whisper, "I've met someone, Delia, and she's great with the girls. Zoe and Dora love her. I think you would too."

He gathered up the suitcases and activity bag and made his way downstairs. This break away from Maddie might be good for both of them, because he wasn't going to let her go. And he needed the next few days away to figure out how to prove to Maddie that he loved her and she could trust him. Because he wanted nothing less than forever.

Maddie had helped her mother make the Thanksgiving meal and it was nearly ready. It was just the four of them—her, her mom, Paul and Pearl. Maddie had brought Pearl in her travel cage since the two of them were staying overnight. Paul didn't seem to mind. In fact, he'd been very gentle with Pearl. So much so, Pearl took to sitting on Paul's shoulder while he watched TV.

"This is nice." Her mother wrapped her arm around Maddie's waist. "Having you stay with us."

The Detroit Lions pregame blared from the living room.

"Yeah." Maddie tipped her head to rest against her mother's.

*Turning the TV down a notch might be nice.*

"Too many holidays without each other," her mom said.

"I know." Stan's fault. He'd never wanted to travel back to Michigan.

Not all Stan's fault. Maddie should have come herself, but she'd never wanted to leave Pearl in Stan's care. She should have packed up Pearl and come home a long time ago. Maybe if she'd trusted her mother enough to help, things might have been different. Maddie might have found protection and, ultimately, a divorce.

She focused on peeling potatoes, recalling her session with Dr. Savannah. The counselor had been great, easy to talk to and understanding, but challenging too. Dr. Savannah had advised Maddie to forgive Stan for what he'd done. If she didn't, she'd continue to see her late husband in every man. She'd continue to give him power over her decisions and relationship choices.

"Smells wonderful, you two. How much longer?" Paul had come into the kitchen and nuzzled her mom's cheek while she basted the turkey.

Her mom batted him away. "Go watch your Lions."

"They're not playing yet." He chuckled, snitched a piece of hot turkey skin and scooted back to the living room.

She watched her mom closely, and her face practically glowed. Maddie hadn't been fair to Paul. She'd put him in the same box as Stan. Paul wasn't Stan. And neither was Jackson. And yet she expected them to behave like Stan and treat her the same way.

Maddie briefly closed her eyes. How long would she continue to let her late husband run her life?

Her mom closed the oven and looked at her. "Maddie, are you okay?"

Maddie had a potato in hand that was partially peeled while she stared off in space, deep in her thoughts. "I just started seeing a counselor."

Her mom's eyes widened. "Oh, honey. I'm so sorry."

Maddie shook her head. "No, this is a good thing. I've been holding on to a lot. There are things I need to let go of and forgive."

"Stan?" her mom asked.

Maddie's mouth dropped open. "How did you know?"

Her mother shrugged. "I didn't. It just seemed odd that since you moved back, you never talked about him. And you haven't put up any pictures of the two of you in your house."

"He didn't hit me, if that's what you're wondering, but he wasn't a good husband." She wasn't going to enlighten her mother about Stan's choke hold. What good would it do?

Her mother stepped close and pulled Maddie into a hug. "I'm so sorry."

Maybe one day she'd tell her mom all of it, but not now, not today. Now that she was finally dealing with the ramifications of her marriage and other deep hurts in her life, she no longer felt so controlled by them.

Dr. Savannah had encouraged her to not only forgive Stan, but to turn all that hurt over to God because she wasn't meant to carry it. She wasn't meant to judge others through broken lenses, and that was what Maddie had been doing, even with her own mother. Keeping everyone at a safe distance in order to protect herself.

Maddie hugged her mother back. "I'm sorry too. I should have come to you sooner."

"Maddie, it's okay. I'm not exactly Mom-of-the-Year."

Maddie laughed. "Why not? I think you're wonderful."

"You are too." Her mom gave her cheek a gentle pinch. "Now let's get these potatoes in the boiling water. The turkey is almost done."

Paul wandered back into the kitchen again. "Anything I can help with?"

"Yes." Her mom loaded her new husband with soft drinks and orders to set them on the dining room table.

"And then I need help peeling potatoes, if you're up for it," Maddie added.

"Put me to work," Paul answered.

Pearl whistled from the living room, then spoke. "Hellloooo, Maddieeeee."

Maddie checked on her really quick, relieved when the parrot didn't look stressed in these new surroundings. "Hello, Pearl."

"Peanuts?"

Maddie chuckled. "No. And I know Paul has given you plenty of cashews."

Maddie was glad she was here. Paul deserved a chance that she hadn't given him. Just because he was a big and brawny man who loved football didn't mean he was a brute.

He came to stand next to her with a paring knife and got busy peeling spuds. Paul was fast too.

"Where'd you learn to peel potatoes like that?"

He gave her a wink. "I know my way around a kitchen. Just wait till you try my homemade stuffed hash browns in the morning."

"After we pick out a Christmas tree."

"What?" Maddie hadn't even thought about Christmas.

She might be moving about that time if her house sold. The sign had gone up in her yard the day before. Her heart pinched every time she thought about moving away from Zoe and Dora.

And Jackson.

Her mom smiled. "I thought it might be nice for the three of us to cut down a pine tree from the woods. With the snow we've gotten, it should be really pretty. And festive."

"That's a great idea." She owed her mom that. Maddie had missed a lot of holidays.

Once the potatoes were boiled and then whipped, Maddie scooped them into a bowl, tossed a large pat of butter in the middle and set the bowl on the dining room table. Paul carved the turkey like a pro and arranged the meat on a platter, which her mom then placed in the middle of the table too.

"Okay, let's eat." Her mom sat down.

Paul had turned the TV down, so when they were all seated, he bowed his head. "Lord, thank You for bringing Maddie to stay with us. Bless this food and our time together. Amen."

It was short and simple, but a heartfelt prayer nonetheless. Maddie glanced at her mom.

Her mother gave her an innocent shrug and passed the cranberry sauce.

Maddie couldn't stop smiling as she filled her plate. Something had changed in her mom and they had a lot of catching up to do. Dinner was a leisurely affair, and Maddie was indeed thankful to get to know her mother's husband a bit better.

After cleanup, Maddie slipped into her coat and ducked outside while her mother and Paul watched the football game. She could hear Pearl squawk every time Paul cheered a play.

Looking up at the darkening sky and the snow falling gently like a picture on a Christmas card, Maddie gave thanks to the Lord. She also asked God to help her forgive Stan.

An image of her mother offering her the cranberry sauce flashed in her mind with brilliant clarity. Was it as simple as that? Offering up her bitterness and hatred like a dish to be passed? It was worth a try.

"Please take it, Lord. I don't want to hold on to it anymore." She meant it.

Maddie stood in her mother's driveway, expecting to feel something more than the snow melting on her cheeks. When she realized she had tears streaming down her cheeks too, Maddie chuckled.

*Thank You, Lord.*

Jackson couldn't wait to get home and start his plan of gently wooing Maddie. Maybe he'd start with candy, then flowers…

It had been a nice Thanksgiving at his parents' place,

but he was glad to get back to a regular routine. One that included Maddie, because the daycare wouldn't have room for Dora until after the New Year.

Driving by her house, he spotted a for-sale sign in her front yard and nearly ran off the road.

"Daddy!" Zoe complained from the back seat.

He looked at her through the rearview mirror. "Sorry. Is your sister still asleep?"

"Yes."

"Then no harm done." Jackson pulled into his driveway and shut off the motor. He leaned his forehead against the steering wheel for a moment, before getting out.

*Why, God?*

Zoe was already out of her booster seat and opening the car door.

"We're going over to Maddie's house." Jackson needed to know why she was selling. Was it because of him? The thought made him sick, and then it made him mad.

"Yay!" Zoe jumped up and down.

Jackson reached in and unbuckled Dora, who slumped forward. He lifted her out and cuddled her against his shoulder.

Zoe had already run next door and stood on Maddie's front stoop. She raised her hand to knock but looked at him for permission.

Jackson nodded. "Go ahead."

Zoe knocked.

And Jackson caught up just as the door opened.

"Hello, Zoe." Maddie peered out and her gaze slammed into his. "Jackson."

"You're selling your house?"

She backed up. "Would you like to come in?"

Jackson brushed past her and laid Dora on the couch.

"Hellloooo." Pearl rang the bell in her cage. The door was open, but the parrot didn't come out.

Zoe knelt down in front of her cage.

"Hello, Pearl," Jackson said, then turned to look at Maddie. "Why?"

She twisted her hands together, but didn't look afraid. She looked more worried than anything. "Remember that boutique in Marquette I told you about?"

"Yeah." He stood in the middle of her living room. There was no way he could sit down until he knew.

Maddie looked at Zoe. "Would you like to get Pearl some chop?"

"Sure." Zoe stood. "Can I take her with me?"

"Yes, as long as it's okay with your dad." Maddie waited for him to respond.

"Yeah, sure. Go ahead, Zoe." Of course it was okay. He knew Zoe was great with the parrot and Pearl was a gentle bird. Why was Maddie double-checking with him? Why was she moving away from them?

"Come, Pearl." Zoe held out her arm.

Sure enough, the parrot climbed out of her cage and flew toward his daughter, landing with precision on Zoe's arm. Then Pearl sidestepped her way up to her shoulder.

Maddie waited for Zoe to enter the kitchen and then she took a step toward him. "I have an opportunity to buy into an expansion of that shop. I'd be part owner and have a designated space for my woolens, as much as I can make."

Jackson spread his arms and his voice rose. "So, why sell your house?"

She shushed him and gave a pointed look at Dora sleeping on the couch before facing him. "For the money. My loan was turned down because even though I put twenty percent down when I bought the house, the bank would only lend up to eighty-five and I don't have enough in savings."

He looked at her, really looked at her, and knew. Candy and flowers were no way to prove his love for her. "How much do you need?"

Maddie's eyes narrowed. "Why?"

Jackson tipped his head to the side. "How much?"

"Thirty thousand."

A tidy sum for sure. "I have it."

Maddie's eyes grew wide.

"I'll give you the money you need."

"You're not serious." She gazed at him with confusion and a little fear.

"Dead serious. You're a good investment," he said, hoping she'd understand he had a lot of faith in her.

"Why would you do that?" she whispered.

He wasn't holding back this time, nor would he use caution. Fool that he was, Jackson bared his heart. "Because I want you to stay here and because I love you."

Maddie let those words wash over her like a soothing cup of chamomile tea. He loved her! And offering to give her the money she needed was definitely proof, but— "I can pay you monthly, you know, like a loan."

Hurt flashed in his eyes before amusement took over. "Is that all you got? I just bared my heart here."

Maddie realized her error and closed the distance between them. "I'm sorry, but I'm a little scared."

He wrapped his arms loosely around her waist. "Why? What scares you, Maddie?"

As she looked into his dear face, Maddie's worries started to melt. She'd learned in grief support group that fears needed to be verbalized in order to deal with them, so she wasn't going to hold back. Not anymore. "I don't think I've ever been in love before. Real love, like I have for you."

Jackson rested his forehead against hers. "I can't promise perfection. I'm going to make mistakes—we both will. But if we choose to trust God and get a little counseling together, I think we'll be good. We'll stay strong."

Maddie's heart sang to hear Jackson talk about trusting God. "I saw Dr. Savannah."

He looked surprised. "You did? When?"

"Tuesday morning, she had a cancellation. Thank you for pushing me to call her. She's great." Maddie had a lot to tell him, but that'd keep for now. For now, she wanted to bask in the warmth of his love and hers.

"So you'll accept my offer and stay?"

Maddie smiled. "If you'll make it a loan, yes."

Jackson grinned. "I have another offer for you, one that I won't ask right away. Know this, Maddie. You are who I want. You. I love who you are and I want us to be forever."

Her throat grew tight and her eyes stung, but she managed to agree. "I'd like that."

"I'd like to kiss you." Jackson tipped up her chin.

It was then that she spotted his bare left hand. She grabbed it. "No ring?"

"I'm not married anymore."

Maddie smiled, reaching for the back of his head to draw him close. "We need to quit talking."

Then she met his lips with her own and kissed him with all her hopes and dreams rolled into one breathless moment. She felt small arms wrapped around her legs and broke away from Jackson.

Maddie looked down to see Dora hugging them both and laughed. "Well, hello, Dora."

Zoe ran from the hallway to join them. She wrapped her arms around them too, but looked up, smiling. "Are you going to marry Daddy?"

Maddie looked at Jackson. Everything was moving so fast, but it felt okay. It felt right.

He shrugged. "Out of the mouths of babes."

There was no sense in denying it. As Jackson had said, they'd work through their past marriages together and come out stronger on the other side. She didn't have to be afraid.

Without looking away from her Romeo's earnest blue eyes, Maddie decided she was done being afraid. "Eventually."

"Yay!" Zoe let go and jumped around.

Dora joined her sister.

And then Pearl flew into the living room to see what was going on. She squawked and then mimicked the girls. "Aaaaaeeeee."

Maddie giggled at the sound. "You realize you're getting a parrot too."

"I wouldn't want it any other way." Jackson pulled her close and rubbed his nose against hers. "I love you and everything that comes with you."

Maddie believed him. She and Pearl were both safe with Jackson Taylor, and with him, Maddie felt like she'd finally come home.

# Epilogue

*Six months later...*

The second weekend in June, after school had let out for summer break, Maddie stood in Jackson's kitchen waiting. She reached to push up her glasses, but they weren't there. She'd switched to contacts for the wedding and was still getting used to them.

She couldn't believe how calm she felt, but then, marrying Jackson was the right thing to do. They had the sincere blessings of their parents and that meant a lot.

Dora and Zoe, both dressed in frilly white dresses, held baskets of peony flower petals ready to throw. They currently twirled in front of her, watching their skirts flutter.

Melanie was already on the back porch waiting for the string quartet to start playing so she could descend the stairs into the backyard.

"You look beautiful, Maddie. That dress is just gorgeous." Her mother stood next to her, ready to walk her down the grassy aisle to meet Jackson and their pastor, who'd marry them.

"Thanks, Mom. You do too." Maddie loved knowing that her mom was finally happy. Not to mention that she and Paul were believers in Christ for their salvation. She and her mother had made up for lost time. They'd grown closer over these last few months than they'd been in years.

With her mom's help, Maddie had sewn her own high-necked, halter-style wedding dress. She'd used layers of the finest dusty pink tulle and covered it with an ivory netting stitched with random shimmers of metallic thread. It was gorgeous material and had taken a lot of time away from her woolens, but it had been worth it.

Her sales were incredible in the Marquette boutique, and Maddie could see herself opening something in Pine one day. She'd have Jackson's huge basement for felting and storing the discarded sweaters she collected far and wide. She'd had an industrial washer and dryer installed with the cash left over from the sale of her house two weeks ago. After she'd paid Jackson back.

He'd had plans drawn up to renovate this very back porch into a large sewing room for her with plenty of room for Pearl. With the southern-facing windows that would be installed, her parrot might prefer her cage here rather than in the living room. Jackson had truly welcomed Pearl into his home and the girls had too.

Maddie and Jackson had decided on a small wedding of just family and friends so they could go to the Bahamas for their honeymoon. Neither had had a proper wedding trip before, so this would be special. Melanie and her husband agreed to stay with the girls and take care of Pearl.

Pearl's outdoor aviary had been moved to Jackson's backyard as well. Maddie and the girls had decorated the outside of it with white ribbons. She heard the parrot whistle and her heart leaped for joy. Jackson hadn't wanted to exclude Pearl from their backyard wedding, complete with a rented event tent for the reception.

The music started and Maddie smiled. "Ready, girls?"

Both stopped twirling.

"We're ready," Zoe said.

Dora stuck her hand in the basket and tossed some peony petals that fluttered to the floor.

Maddie laughed. "Not yet, sweetie. Wait until we're outside."

Her bridal bouquet was a simple bundle of light and dark pink peonies they'd picked this morning from a line of bushes growing along the other side of the house. Their soft scent would always remind Maddie of this day. Her real wedding day.

Melanie walked down the steps and the girls followed their aunt exactly as they'd rehearsed last night.

The music changed and it was Maddie's turn to walk out into the sunshine. The warmth of the sun washed over her as she stood on the back porch.

Jackson spotted her and grinned.

She smiled back. He looked handsome in a tan suit and matching pink tie. Her very own Romeo.

On her mother's arm, Maddie walked the aisle strewn with peony petals between rows of white chairs. The whole way, she kept her gaze firmly fixed on Jackson, who never once looked away, even though Melanie's husband, standing up as best man, poked Jackson with his elbow.

When Maddie finally made it to his side, she gripped his hand like she'd never let go.

"We are gathered here today," Pastor Parsons began.

Jackson leaned toward her and whispered, "You're beautiful."

"You are too."

The pastor gave them a pointed look. "Are we ready?" The guests tittered.

"I've never been more ready in my life," Maddie answered, which made their guests laugh again and Jackson grin even wider.

It was true. Maddie looked forward to a life with her new family and loved ones without an ounce of fear.

Today, they pledged their lives together as man and wife before God. They promised to love and honor each other while placing their trust wholly in the Lord.

Maddie had never been happier, nor more at peace. She had a lot of living to catch up on, and seeing her future stretch before her, she knew it was going to be good.

\* \* \* \* \*

*If you enjoyed this Second Chance Blessings*
*story by Jenna Mindel, be sure to pick up*
*the first book in this miniseries:*

A Secret Christmas Family

*Available now from Love Inspired!*

Dear Reader,

Thank you so much for reading Maddie's story—the second book in the Second Chance Blessings series. I hope you have enjoyed her journey to wholeness and real love with her hero named Jackson.

Maddie's character came to me as you see her—withdrawn and hiding behind those giant eyeglasses. But I didn't know why. Finding those reasons came bit by bit as I wrote this story.

Creating a character is a lot like putting together a puzzle. With time and plenty of *whys*, those odd little pieces fit in place to become a hero and heroine. Maddie's puzzle was a tough one to write because she was emotionally damaged, and Jackson had been through the wringer as well, considering his wife's suicide. Even though he went for counseling, which is wise, he refused to trust God.

Suicide is ravaging our country. According to the CDC, "In 2020, suicide was among the top 9 leading causes of death for people ages 10–64. Suicide was the second leading cause of death for people ages 10–14 and 25–34." There are hotlines that can help in that terrible moment of consideration. Text 988 for the Suicide and Crisis Lifeline.

There is a lot of pain and hopelessness out there, but God can take our damage if we're willing to let go of it. I mean, really let go. And that's His promise to us—peace beyond understanding. He's only a prayer away.

I love to hear from readers. You can drop a note in the mail to PO Box 2075, Petoskey MI 49770, or check out my website, www.jennamindel.com, which has a newsletter sign-up and link to my author Facebook page.

Erica's second chance is next… Stay tuned!

*Jenna*

## HIS FORGOTTEN AMISH LOVE
### by Rebecca Kertz
Two years ago, David Troyer asked to court Fannie Miller...then disappeared without a trace. Suddenly he's back with no memory of her, and she's tasked with catering his family reunion. Where has he been and why has he forgotten her? Will her heart be broken all over again?

## THE AMISH SPINSTER'S DILEMMA
### by Jocelyn McClay
When a mysterious *Englisch* granddaughter is dropped into widower Thomas Reihl's life, he turns to neighbor Emma Beiler for help. The lonely spinster bonds with the young girl and helps Thomas teach her their Amish ways. Can they both convince Thomas that he needs to start living—and loving—again?

## A FRIEND TO TRUST
### *K-9 Companions* • by Lee Tobin McClain
Working at a summer camp isn't easy for Pastor Nate Fisher. Especially since he's sharing the director job with standoffish Hayley Harris. But when Nate learns a secret about one of their campers that affects Hayley, he'll have to decide if their growing connection can withstand the truth.

## THE COWBOY'S LITTLE SECRET
### *Wyoming Ranchers* • by Jill Kemerer
Struggling cattle rancher Austin Watkins can't believe his son's nanny is quitting. Cassie Berber wants to pursue her dreams in the big city—even though she cares for the infant and his dad. Can Austin convince her to stay and build a home with them in Wyoming?

## LOVING THE RANCHER'S CHILDREN
### *Hope Crossing* • by Mindy Obenhaus
Widower Jake Walker needs a nanny for his kids. But with limited options in their small town, he turns to former friend Alli Krenek. Alli doesn't want anything to do with the single dad, but when she finds herself falling for his children, she'll try to overcome their past and see what the future holds...

## HIS SWEET SURPRISE
### by Angie Dicken
Returning to his family's orchard, Lance Hudson is seeking a fresh start. He never expects to be working alongside his first love, single mom Piper Gray. When Piper reveals she's the mother of a child he never knew about, Lance must decide if he'll step up and be the man she needs.

---

**LOOK FOR THESE AND OTHER LOVE INSPIRED BOOKS WHEREVER BOOKS ARE SOLD, INCLUDING MOST BOOKSTORES, SUPERMARKETS, DISCOUNT STORES AND DRUGSTORES.**

LICNM0423

# HARLEQUIN
## PLUS

Try the best multimedia subscription service for romance readers like you!

---

## **Read, Watch and Play.**

Experience the easiest way to get the romance content you crave.

Start your **FREE TRIAL** at
<u>www.harlequinplus.com/freetrial</u>.